Praise for *Our Kind*

"[W]ry and compressed, full of quick, telling details. . . . I can't think of another contemporary novel except James Salter's *Light Years* that so zealously grapples with the passage of time as a subject. . . . [S]tartling and cumulative [in its] heft."

—Jennifer Egan, *The New York Times Book Review*

"[T]he 1950s women of . . . *Our Kind* are a dying breed; but [Walbert] insists, rightly, on the viability of their ambition-nipped lives."

—*The Village Voice*

"Wry observations, witty insights, and pithy descriptions capture a specific society but tell us all something about our own."

—*The Charlotte Observer*

"There's no denying Walbert's talent—or her ambition."

—*Newsday*

"[C]ombines a wistful lyricism with wry humor. . . . Walbert's keen-eyed social observations (not unlike Jane Austen's) . . . really sparkle."

—Amanda Kolson Hurley, *The Washington Times*

"Brilliant [and] moving. . . . Walbert's characters are caught like insects in amber as they make late-in-life discoveries no school could ever teach. Brittle, funny and poignant, this is a prickly treat."

—*Publishers Weekly* (starred review)

"Walbert adores her characters, and as a result, they're . . . giddy, resilient possessors of a girlish beauty. They have a blast; the reader does too."

—*Organic Style*

"Kate Walbert's dazzling novel has the elegiac grace and wisdom— and also the wistfulness—of a John Cheever story. . . . What a marvelous book."

—Katharine Weber, author of
The Music Lesson and *The Little Women*

Praise for *The Gardens of Kyoto*

"Elusive, eloquent . . . with understated power."

—*The New York Times*

"In precise, delicate prose, the author renders with equal power the quiet desperation of a girl growing up in 1950s America and the ethereal."

—*The New Yorker*

"Readers in love with language will adore this book."

—*USA Today*

"An exquisite novel of love, loss, and memory."

—Ann Packer, author of *The Dive from Clausen's Pier*

Our Kind

· A NOVEL ·

KATE WALBERT

Scribner

New York   London   Toronto   Sydney

SCRIBNER
1230 Avenue of the Americas
New York, NY 10020

Copyright © 2004 by Kate Walbert

First Scribner trade paperback edition 2005

SCRIBNER and design are trademarks of Macmillan Library Reference USA, Inc., used under license by Simon & Schuster, the publisher of this work.

For information about special discounts for bulk purchases, please contact Simon & Schuster Special Sales: 1-800-456-6798 or business@simonandschuster.com

Designed by Kyoko Watanabe
Text set in Berling

Manufactured in the United States of America

1 3 5 7 9 10 8 6 4 2

Library of Congress Control Number: 2003066294

ISBN 0-7432-4559-8
0-7432-4560-1 (Pbk)

"The Intervention" originally appeared in *The Paris Review*.

"Question in a Field" from *Collected Poems: 1922–1953* by Louise Bogan. Copyright © 1954 by Louise Bogan. Copyright renewed 1982 by Maidie Alexander Scannell. Reprinted by permission of Farrar, Straus and Giroux, LLC.

FOR MY MOTHER

CONTENTS

Question in a Field

Pasture, stone wall, and steeple,
What most perturbs the mind:
The heart-rending homely people,
Or the horrible beautiful kind?

Louise Bogan

The Intervention

It was one of those utterances that sparkled—the very daring! Could you see us? Canoe shrugged, to be expected. After all, Canoe was our local recovering; it was she who left those pamphlets in the clubhouse next to the men's Nineteenth Hole.

Still, the very daring!

Intervention.

Canoe cracked her knuckles, lit a cigarette. We sat by her swimming pool absentmindedly pulling weeds from around the flagstones. The ice of our iced tea had already melted into water and it was too cold to swim, besides.

"It's obvious," Canoe said, blowing. "He's going to kill himself in less than a month. I don't want that blood on my hands."

Who would?

He was someone we loved. Someone we could not help but love. A colleague of our ex-husbands, a past encounter. We had known Him since before we were we, from our first weeks in this town, early summers. We loved His hair.

Golden. The color of that movie actor's hair, the famous one. Sometimes we caught just the gleam of it through the windshield of his BMW as He drove by. Sporty. Waving. Green metallic, leather interior. Some sort of monogram on the wheel. You've seen the license plate? SOLD. A realtor, but never desperate. Yes, He sold our Mimi Klondike's Tudor on Twelve Oaks Lane with full knowledge of her rotting foundation. But desperate? No. Just thirsty.

"Intervention," Barbara repeated. Canoe flexed her toes as if she had invented the word.

This a late summer day, a fallish day. Ricardo, the pool boy, swept maple leaves from the pool water, in this light a dull, sickly yellow. We watched him; we couldn't take our eyes off. Canoe interrupted.

"Actually, I shouldn't be the one explaining. There's someone from the group who's our expert. Pips Phelp, actually."

Pips Phelp? The lawyer? Pips Phelp?

We spoke in whispers. Who knew who lived in trees?

Besides, He might drive up any minute. He often did. You'd hear the crunch of His tires on the gravel, see the flash of blond hair behind the windshield. These times you'd dry your hands on your shirtfront, check your face in the toaster. You wouldn't want to be caught, what? Alone? You let Him in. He'd ask you to. He would stand at your door, behind your screen, wondering if He could. Of course, you'd say, though you looked a mess. If you were unlucky, the dishwasher ran. One of the louder cycles. If you were lucky, all was still—the house in magical order, spotless, clean. He surveyed; this was his job. You never knew, He told you, when He might be needed.

You shivered. Him a handsome man. A man with the habit of standing close, His smell: animal, rooty—your hands after gardening. His straight teeth were white, though He didn't smile that way. His was a better smile, toothless, brief, as if He understood He had caught you with more than a wet shirtfront. You obliged the suspicion. You were always guilty of something.

Still, you showed Him what you had done, were attempting. Recent renovations. Whatnot. A fabric swatch laid on the back of your couch. A roll of discount wallpaper for the powder room, shells of some sort. You'd been trying, you'd explain, to fix the place up. But things had gotten behind; the contractor's attentions divided, et cetera, et cetera.

He nodded, or did not. His was a serious business: assessing value. Worth.

———

Ricardo, the pool boy, served sandwiches. We had spent a few days per Canoe's instruction, contemplating the responsibility of our action: the absolute commitment, the difficulty, the discipline, the *sacrifice*. Esther Curran now sat among us. Someone had invited her. She was speaking of how He had shown her a Cape near Grendale Knoll after Walter's death, when she had believed she couldn't bear it— the house, the reminders—and how she, Esther, was no longer a beautiful woman. Here Esther peeled the crust off her sandwich and looked away.

We sat around her in Canoe's wrought-iron; it was too

cold to lounge. The weather had suddenly turned, and the reason we sat around the pool at all was beyond us, unless it had something to do with Ricardo. We watched him receding toward the pool house then turned back to Esther.

This was the point, Esther was saying, though we may have lost it.

He had taken her hand. He had stroked it. He had told her of the possibilities. There wasn't much to be done—the demolition of the Florida room, a few shingles rehung, refurbishing the kitchen. Think of it, He had told her.

We watched Esther with looks on our faces. We had never understood her. Rich as Croesus, she drove a Dodge and compared prices at the Safeway. Her husband, Walter, had died years ago, but she still referred to him as if he had run downtown for milk and would be back any minute. She allowed her hair to gray, her nails to go ragged. True, she had always been our eccentric—an artist, she kept chameleons in her living room draperies and would often arrive at parties with paint on her hands—but more than once in recent years, we understood, she had been escorted in the early hours of the morning, found wandering in robe and slippers on the old Route 32, luckily rarely traveled, for she could have been struck down as easily as a stray dog.

Now here she was among us.

"*Intervention,*" she said, "is not a word of which I am particularly fond." Esther cut her crustless sandwich into nine even squares. "Walter and I are of the live-and-let-live philosophy," she continued, "but in certain unavoidable circumstances, such as the one we confront here today, I say, yes. I say, intervene." She picked up a square and we waited, thinking Esther might have more to add, but she simply smiled and popped it whole into her mouth.

"Frankly," Canoe said, this to Pips Phelp, who had convened the meeting and sat at the edge of us in a deck chair, "I don't want to hear about Him wrapped around a telephone pole. I wouldn't be able to live with myself."

Pips Phelp nodded. We knew him from the Club, one of a number of men who zipped by in a cart heading elsewhere, gloved hand guiding the wheel. He seemed to have little to say, too quiet for an interventionist, though Canoe insisted he was skilled in these matters. And we had read in the literature that we needed him: a leader, a discussion initiator.

"Understood," he said.

———

We agreed to meet the next day in the Safeway parking lot for a run-through. Pips Phelp would play His part. Did we understand fully, Pips had explained, that this would be tantamount to ambush? There would be little time, he said. He will fight you. He will want to flee. He will deny your accusations. You will have to talk quickly. Under absolutely no circumstance can you allow Him to leave the vehicle. (We had decided that this would be the place we'd find Him.) When it is over, one of you will get behind the wheel and drive Him to the Center. You will check Him in. It has been arranged.

Pips Phelp now sat in his Buick, the motor running. We

saw him clearly though we pretended not to: This was part of the plan. We pulled in in Viv's Suburban and got out one at a time, no one saying a word. Canoe gave a short whistle and we circled the Buick, feeling the rush of the boarding-school escapade. What were we doing? Was anyone watching?

Pips Phelp pretended not to notice. He was a poor substitute for Him, truth be told. He sat there in a gut-hold against the wheel, his fingers strumming. He smelled of gum, or mints, of pretzels, of efforts to stave off tobacco. We knew him as a weak man. We knew him as a man who could be trusted. His wife, Eleanor, carried the look of the perpetually bored; his children were overachievers. You can only guess at the good-cheer stickers on the bumper of his Buick. He was a hedge trimmer, a leaf raker, a model-boat builder; he was a man who never thought of selling. Every spring along the borders of the driveway to his house—a ranch just past the K&O Cemetery—he planted red and pink impatiens.

"Pips!" This from Canoe, acting surprised, our signal to converge. Pips looked up, turned off the engine. "Canoe!" he said, our signal to open his doors. Canoe had already slid in the passenger side, yanked the keys from the ignition. Our hearts beat too loud, drumlike. We were not used to intervening.

"What is this?" Pips said. "What's everybody doing here?" His talent was not for acting. He sounded like a commercial you might see on late-night television.

"We're here because we love you," Canoe said. "We're here because we care about your life."

We flushed. Who wouldn't? We didn't care for Pips's life.

We wanted Him. We wanted His smooth leather shoes, His argyle socks, His blue cashmere double-breasted coat. We wanted His promise of future appreciation.

"What are you talking about?" Pips said, shifting around to look at those of us in the backseat. Some couldn't fit and leaned on the windows. "What's the big idea?"

We laughed; we couldn't help it. "Please, Pips," Viv said to clue him in. "He'd never say 'big idea.'"

Pips gave us a look and turned back toward the windshield. He composed himself, a man of infinite patience, then shifted around again. "What's the meaning of this?" he said.

"The meaning," said Viv, "is concern. You are a sick person. It's not your fault. You can't help yourself. It's genetic. You need help. We're here to help you."

Some of us bit our fingernails.

Pips laughed like Bela Lugosi. "Sick? Me? What do you mean by these unfounded accusations. I've never felt better. I think you're sick. I think you are all suffering from a serious mental health problem."

This was going all wrong. No one sounded like a real person.

"What we're trying to say," said Judy Sawyer, but she didn't know what. Then came a long and awkward pause. Canoe sighed, audibly. "Come on, ladies," she said. "We've gotten off on the wrong foot." Then she opened the passenger side and got out, signaling for us to do the same. We did, as Pips Phelp waited, pretending, once again, that he had just driven up.

Know that we are a close-knit community. We've lived here for years, which is not to say that our ancestors are buried here; simply, this is the place we have all ended up. We were married in 1953. Divorced in 1976. Our grown daughters pity us; our grown sons forget us. We have grandchildren we visit from time to time, but their manners agitate, so we return, nervous, thankful to view them at a distance.

Most of us excel at racquet sports.

It is not in our makeup to intervene. This goes against the grain, is entirely out of our character. We allow for differences, but strive not to show them. Ours are calm waters, smooth sailing. Yes, some among us visit therapists, but, quite frankly, we believe this is a passing phase, like our former passion for fondue, or our semester learning decoupage.

We've seen a lot. We've seen the murder-suicide of the Clifford Jacksons, Tate Kieley jailed for embezzlement, Dorothy Schoenbacher in nothing but a mink coat in August dive from the roof of the Cooke's Inn. We've seen Dick Morehead arrested in the ladies' dressing room at Lord & Taylor, attempting to squeeze into a petite teddy. We've seen Francis Stoney gone mad, Brenda Nelson take to cocaine. We've seen the blackballing of the Stewart Collisters. We've seen more than our share of liars and cheats, thieves. Drunks? We couldn't count.

Still, He's someone we love. And, in truth, we love few.

Early the morning after our practice run, we met again at the Safeway. Canoe brought a thermos of coffee and we stood drinking from our styrofoam cups in the early cold as if at a tailgate. It did seem a game, the weather, football weather, changeable, ominous, geese honking overhead, flying else-where. A strong wind set loose shopping carts in random directions, as if they were being pushed by the ghosts of shoppers past. Coupon offers and flyers of various sorts blew about as well. Canoe suggested coffee cake, but we declined. We were, on the whole, nervous. We enjoyed our weekly stocking up at the Safeway; we kept lists. But to linger in its parking lot felt just shy of delinquency and a long way from Canoe's swimming pool and Ricardo's languid strokes. When we finally spotted Pips Phelp's Buick turning in, our spirits had undeniably flagged.

Pips didn't seem to notice. "Ladies," he said, slamming the door, getting out. "Top of the morning!"

Was this man always working from some sort of script?

"Why the long faces?" he said.

"They'll get over it," Canoe said. She dropped her styro-foam cup to the asphalt and crushed it, twisting her flat as if to stub out a cigarette butt. We watched, riveted. You do not need to tell us we were stalling. Canoe got into her Jeep and rolled down the window. "Understand," she told him, "they're not used to unpleasantness."

We have seen a lot, it's true, but know so little. How were we to learn? Years ago we were led down the primrose lane, then abandoned somewhere near the carp pond. Suffice it to say there is little nourishment here and the carp have grown strange cancers. When we look in their pond we see them beneath our own watery faces.

But think of the consequence: His disappearance.

We piled in as instructed. We buckled our safety belts. We turned to Pips Phelp, who stood in salute, and waved. Canoe gunned the Jeep. "Hi-ho, Silver," she said, and we were off, the plan to find Him come hell or high water, to drive to the limits of our town, to cover His turf. We watched Pips Phelp trail us in his Buick, his flaccid pink face in the rearview. We weren't nice. We made fun. We said how ordinary was Pips, how completely known. We said how He could flatten Pips Phelp with one fist.

"Kaboom!" Barbara shouted. And she meant it. "Kaboom! Kaboom!" She raised her fist and punched the air.

"Why the anger?" Mimi Klondike asked, as if intervention were catching.

Barbara shrugged. "Felt like it?" she said.

Esther, we noticed, didn't speak. She wasn't often of late among us, and now she might as well not have been. She sat in the back of the Jeep staring out the window, some kind of smock we wouldn't be caught dead in spread over her legs. She had letters in her pockets to people we had never met; her hair seemed unwashed.

"Esther?" Mimi Klondike said. "Why the long face?" Barbara smirked, but Esther simply turned toward us. She might have been smiling, or this might have been her natural expression. Beyond her, our country—changing maples, stone walls, gravel drives, newly washed automobiles, children, horses, dogs—passed. But we were looking at Esther.

"I was thinking how strange," she finally said. "I was think-ing how strange to be alive." Then she turned away. We drove in silence; what else was there to do? Time passed and we thought our thoughts; we thought of Him. How He held a flashlight to our souls, our basements. How He checked for dry rot, carpenter ants, the carcasses of flying insects. In the darkness we saw Him searching, and we yelled down, Do you need a hand?

"Bingo!" Canoe shouted. She slammed the Jeep brake. "Bingo bango!"

We leaned in, looking. "What?" we said. "Him?"

Yes, there: Pinned to Louise Cooper's chemicled lawn, the sign: SOLD REALTORS, freshly hammered into the ground. Beside it his BMW, forest green, buffed as his nails, stood idle in Louise's drive, arriving or leaving impossible to say. Henry Cooper, on early retirement, had recently dropped dead putting the eighteenth green. We knew Louise had thoughts of moving to Captiva. Still, we felt the jealousy of His trans-ferred affections. Louise? we thought. Her?

"Keep calm!" Canoe shouted, veering in. Our hands were in our laps, our feet pushed against the carpeted floor, brak-ing. Mimi and Barbara ducked on impulse. The rest of us sat stock-still. We knew the plan: Pips Phelp would stay behind, at a distance, there if needed, ready to follow in his car to the Center, to do the necessary paperwork to check Him in. The approvals had been given, the gears were in motion.

Canoe parked the Jeep, jerked the emergency brake. This a stroke of luck, really. We might have found Him nowhere. We might have been too late. Now here we were—sitting and listening to the ticking engine, watching the steam rise off the hood. The day seemed warmer, the gray breaking into blue, the sun a sudden glare. It shone off the chrome of His BMW, flashed in our eyes as if a badge He held up for protection. Was He there? Did we see Him?

Canoe got out. She slammed the front door and sauntered over. She strode, Canoe, the toughest among us. We kept quiet. We waited for the signal: two coughs followed by a hand clap. This would mean He was in the vehicle and we should proceed as rehearsed. Mimi, still ducking, rolled down her window so we could hear better, but what we heard was an ordinary day: a dog barking, crickets, a siren at the far edge of town. In it Canoe's boots crunched gravel; Canoe knocked.

———

It should be said that in recent months He had acquired a new BMW. The latest model. Understand Him as a leaser. In His profession, the importance of the vehicle is not to be underestimated. Every year He trades up. Still, the license plate remains: SOLD. The color, forest green. This one, however, has been slightly altered—the windows blackened, as if a rebuke to our constant attentions.

But He cannot escape us. We know His comings and goings, His ring size. We know at the Stone Barn He orders Manhattan clam chowder, a cup, and a grilled cheese for lunch. We know His difficulty with languages, His general insecurity in all things pertaining to math. We know as a boy He watched the mayor hide the golden Easter egg then blatantly pretended to find it. We know He dreams of killing. We know He scratches himself in ugly places and picks His nose; that His breath is rank in the morning and He scissors black hairs from His ears and plucks His eyebrows.

We know this and more: His bad back, His quenchless thirst. He is our faithless husband, our poor father. He is our bad son, our schemer, our rogue. He is our coward in the conflict, our liar. He has betrayed all He has promised.

Still, we love Him.

———

"Must be in the house," Canoe shouts back to us. "Come on."

We go. We fan out. Our hearts taut drums. Our feet heavy. Canoe crouches ahead, then rounds the bend, breaking away from the cul-de-sac. We run after her and line up on either side—Barbara at the far end, Mimi, the near. We cross our arms over our chests and wait. Canoe tries the front door. It's open. She pushes through. It is Louise Cooper's house, but it may as well be our own—the powder room off the foyer, Louise's monogrammed hand towels. There's Ivory soap in the shape of shells, dirtied from her gardener's hands. There's a chandelier that's dusty, unused; unpaid bills on the secretary. A needlepoint giraffe, weighted with sand, holds the den door open. Here we'd find Louise's real life: her *TV Guides*, her tarnished tennis trophies, framed photographs of her children with outdated hairstyles. But we're not going there. We pause, instead, in the empty foyer. What are we listening for? What do we want?

And then we hear Him. He is speaking in a low voice, a whisper. It is a sound we'd recognize anywhere: the sound of Him prospecting. A cold call. Like the slap of waves in our ocean, like a salt cure. He wants something. He is asking. To all of us He has spoken in such a manner, kissed our fingers. He has guided us through our living rooms, His hand on the small of our backs.

"Shhhhh," Canoe says, as if someone has spoken. But no one has said a word. We simply stand at the bottom of Louise Cooper's staircase like bridesmaids waiting to catch the bouquet, but we are not bridesmaids. We are women near the end of our lives. We look up at nothing: the hallway, the bedroom doors.

Still, His voice is everywhere. Which room? Which direction? Canoe climbs. We follow. At the top of the stairs, we pause, waiting. Nothing. No sound at all but something just below the surface quiet. What? Something so familiar: a woman weeping? Our Louise? We walk down the hallway, pushing at doors—there are so many empty bedrooms. This one simply light from the now-blue sky shining through its open windows onto the poplin spread, pulled taut, pillows fluffed as if Louise is expecting guests; the next one, the same. We move quickly. We hurry. We push on doors, we open closets.

We do not find her until the maid's room. She sits on a narrow cot among little artifacts—a wire-cage mannequin, a yellow-painted dresser, a children's mirror. On the floor there is no rug. If we were barefoot we would be splintered, but we are not. We are shoed and zipped, buttoned and cov-

ered; this we notice because Louise is not. She is without a
stitch of clothing, entirely nude.

She covers herself when we burst in, drawing her legs up
and arms around to cinch them. She is a ball of flesh, Louise
Cooper, leaking from the eyes. She does not need to ask to
know our mission; she points, weakly, in the direction of a
narrow staircase—the back way. Esther takes the lead and
we hurry, pell-mell, reckless. We sense there is little time and
so we tumble down the stairs, our flats nicking the soft
wood, our hands slapping cold walls. Released near the back
door into the open—the sudden fresh air, the sudden light—
we run. We tear. We might spread our arms. Fly.

We head out so fast our flats flapped off some way back,
seven pair abandoned like fourteen blackbirds in a jagged line,
our soft soles hopscotching gravel, rock, then the grassy stub-
ble in the field behind the Coopers', Esther ripping the just-
red stalks from their roots, Barbara and Mimi holding hands,
running, Viv and Judy behind, Canoe in the lead. We must
find Him, we know. We must intervene. We do not want Him
wrapped around a telephone pole. We do not want that blood
on our hands. We must save Him, mustn't we? We must save
Him, quick.

But first, no. First, we must save ourselves.

Esther's Walter

You could say we had never understood Esther Curran, though we adored her, nonetheless. She lived in a tumble-down house off the old Route 32, a house that had been, when her husband, Walter, was alive, a showpiece of our county. Andrew Wyeth himself had knocked on their door one winter morning, asking if he might walk their fields and sketch.

"I can still see the man," Esther would recount in the telling. "As ordinary as you and me, a regular gentleman, not as handsome as Walter, but kind in the eyes."

Here we would smile. Esther's Walter had been the very definition of homely, the least enviable of our men. Indeed, if we were to rank the husbands—as sometimes, in the early years of our first marriages, we would suggest—Trip Goodrich inevitably sailed to the top and he, Walter Curran, sank to the bottom. Still, Esther worshipped him in death as in life, speaking of him in the present tense and, from time to time, wearing his picture tied with twine around her neck.

Should it truly have surprised us?

We received the invitation as one receives invitations to any event: cotillion, the Bachelors' Ball, one of our children marrying or announcing the birth of a child. She requested our company, she wrote, on the anniversary of Walter's death. Please bring a covered dish, she wrote. Surprise in store!

We puzzled over the invitation, the exclamation point intriguing though easily misleading. We use punctuation with abandon, our pocketbooks stuffed with histrionic grocery and to-do lists—onions???!!!!; CLEANERS!! Still, our minds raced!

———

Was it years since we'd seen Esther? Oh, the Intervention, of course, and here and there before; ours a small town. We would occasionally bump into her in the Rite Aid or the john of the Rusty Scupper. But those Esther meetings were by chance, not plan, and so we tended to mumble greetings and move on, our hands gripping the smooth bar of the shopping cart, or crumpling the square of brown paper towel into a ball. Was it that we didn't understand her, or that we understood her too well? All we knew was that she had long declined our invitations. Regretfully. And chitchat had never interested her. Once she had been the artist of our group; she spoke Italian like a native, trained at a finishing school next to a lake in Switzerland.

But Esther now seemed a different animal, ethereal in a way we'd never be: one foot in the Safeway, one foot in the next world.

Let it be said that we have always understood the notion of privacy.

Let it be said that we do not like to interfere.

If a woman is willingly alone in a tumbledown house off the old Route 32; if trash has collected in the muddied ruts of her drive and the garden's yarrow grown to the height of a man, it is, presumably, her business. If she has been found, once or twice, wandering in robe and slippers toward the Grange Hall, her hands kneading shreds of used tissue in her pockets, her fingernails dirty, she is perfectly capable, we'd agree, of pulling herself back up by her bootstraps.

Lord knows we have all had our difficulties.

———

She answered the door with dried flowers tucked behind her ears. Truly. Shoeless. We pretended not to notice, breezing in with our covered dishes; it might have been yesterday when we were last here, at one of her Christmas teas—the children in their pinafores, curtseying greetings then running off to pull the tails from the poor chameleons trapped in the draperies. Or a Labor Day softball game, when the fields around Esther's property erupted in goldenrod.

(She had never had them, children, though she loved them nonetheless, loved ours, particularly, remembering their birthdays, their middle names. It was to Esther that Lizzie Cooper turned after the Colin Cemetery fiasco; and there were many times when we'd startle to see one of our girls sitting with Esther in Brainard's Park—she had been sketching something, been caught unawares though she quickly put it aside—heads bent in consultation of God knows what.)

It might have been just last week that we played rummy in her foyer, the card tables set with baskets of gourds and turkeys constructed out of playing cards, pinched into form by spray-painted clothespins. Gold. Or arrived for her costume ball, our costumes consisting of masks and boas, cheerleading skirts and saddle shoes, or hippie wigs; hers a scarecrow, straw stuffed into brassiere and panties so that it itched like a sonofabitch, she announced, smiling, teeth blackened with mascara.

She was the artist in our midst, though she claimed to only be tinkering. Walter is the talent, she'd say of his sculptures— what looked to us like molten lead, rusted, twisted; we could never find the form though we had tried. Esther walking us from piece to piece, Walter's work displayed on what looked to be every flat surface in the house and even on the crest of the field beyond—a slice of steel curled into the shape of a shell, like something washed up from a distant ocean. His tour de force, Esther called it. His greatest inspiration. Apparently, he had settled on sculpture, despite his musical talents, during one of his childhood bouts with malaria, drawing elaborate ideas for constructions in the twelve notebooks Esther donated after his death to our library. Gay Burt had once, as a lark, checked them out, though she couldn't make heads or tails, she said, except for the note she had found folded on the back page of Journal V, written in Walter's strange, plodding hand. Darling, it read. Tonight, tonight.

But years had passed.

We told Esther she had never looked better. So relaxed! Rested!

In truth, in the harshness of the indoor light Esther looked oddly stricken by age, as if it had descended on her overnight: the dried lavender flowers the only color against her face. What we remembered as green eyes were something just shy of beige, and her nose, once fine, looked bulbous and hard. She could have used some work but she wasn't the type. She smiled and ushered us in.

There was the smell of cats, and dogs underfoot and rivets throughout her stained walls; one could imagine the ping of a light hammer would send the plaster down in a great mushrooming cloud. Indeed the entire house appeared as if it could wash away with the next hard rain.

"Look at the place!" we said. "Look!"

We were once rich, or close enough. Our husbands had good jobs, buying and selling. We left them some years ago in a thundering of hooves, our long faces uncompromised by apology. They would remarry, mostly, younger girls or women not our type.

We couldn't have cared less. We kept the house and the pool, occasionally a court. We drew together. Afternoons at the Club for nine holes, evenings at the Delphi, listening to lectures: the architecture of the Prairie School, that sort of thing. In the earlier years, mornings were at Canoe's, weather permitting, the children friends and old enough to entertain themselves.

Now "Marco? Polo!" lilts in the distance like a departing train, familiar and expected, too far away to catch.

Where has the time gone?

Of Esther Curran we knew this: Walter had whisked her off her feet, quite literally, saving her from a runaway bus that would surely have mowed her down in its path. The driver crashed into a cable car, killing only himself though disrupting service throughout San Francisco for the rest of the day. This happened in that city, exotic and too far west: the land of fruits and nuts.

Esther had been with her father, a notorious drunk who would die alone in a restaurant, choking on a piece of steak.

We knew this and the rest of it: the orphaned mother—a charity case at Miss Porter's—whose beauty transfixed anyone who happened to stumble upon it, which Harry, Esther's father, certainly did: stoned from the minute he laid eyes on her. In the back issues of certain newspapers the two of them waltz at charity functions, Esther's mother with gloves up to her elbows, and hair, a white-blond, twisted into a chignon, her neck and shoulders marble-smooth; Harry leaning against her, his cummerbund cinched.

———

You need not tell us Esther's story is absurd, a fairy tale: girl of eighteen, a debutante, fresh from a finishing school next to a lake in Switzerland, its church spire, if we imagined it, reflected in the sheen of the surface that always sheened, given the nature of the blue sky and the tranquillity of the seasons, there, where girls like Esther recited Italian with perfect accents, peeling grapes; a girl with hair as white-blond as her mother's saved by a boy so homely he might have been beautiful, his buckteeth biting down hard as he struggled to lay her gently onto the sidewalk, his eyes distorted by an overactive thyroid, or under. Who knew which and did it matter? He was sickly from the get-go, his sallow skin pale and his hair already thinning.

And was she all right?

Yes, yes, she was fine.

Could he escort her to a bench?

No, no, her father was right here.

But Harry had slipped out as the careening bus careened on, his daughter safely in the arms of another man. Harry needed a drink. He needed to escape his watchdog daughter, kidnapping him to this godforsaken coast. He needn't be told what to do; he knew exactly. He needed a drink. Perhaps several. He'd find her, eventually: The crowd had the look of staying and she seemed comfortable in that gentleman's arms.

And so Harry disappeared and left Esther in Walter's charge.

Her knight in shining armor. My hero, she'd say. This Gay Burt reported later, having witnessed it herself: Esther into her cups at the Bottle and Cork, a paper cocktail napkin pinched to the top of her head as if a bow. "My hero," she said, the little napkin forgotten, still balanced on her head as Esther reached for a pretzel.

"I'm famished," Suzie said, because she usually was, because we had been milling around Esther's living room with not a cracker in sight. Esther's rescued greyhound, the one called Goneril, slept on its ugly, narrow back, legs up like a dead possum. Reputation for kindness and loyalty, et cetera, et cetera; we did our best to ignore its birdy haunches, branded with a strange symbol; its bright pink eyes, minuscule in that long, bony head.

We were hungry; *starved.* We could have roasted the thing, picked clean its bones.

The grandfather clock ticked; the draperies, where in earlier times the chameleons—three known as the Gorgons— skirted from blue cord to brown velvet, hung as if discouraged. No doubt the mongrels had crushed the poor Gorgons, swallowed them whole, and the velvet has not been washed for years.

"It used to be French blue," Louise Cooper ventured.

We looked at her.

"The divan."

"I remember it as rose," Judy Sawyer said. "A blush."

"I promise you, it was blue."

"I don't remember that at all," Judy said, because she wouldn't. Her mind seemed to be going—where, we couldn't always tell—and lately she dragged one foot; now she sat at the edge of us entirely overdressed, a long strand of pearls looped around her neck, and pumps.

"At one of the parties, Lizzie blanched all over it," Louise Cooper said. "Ruined her dress and shoes.

"They spiked the punch," she said.

"Henry gave her the hairbrush. Bristle side," she said, at which point Esther's voice rang out among us. "What a night, Walter!"

We sat very still.

Esther stood at the threshold to the dining room, lit now with candles, shadowy. We could see a large portrait of Walter over the table, his hands clasped and no doubt yellowed by the malaria. He'd contracted it in Brazil, apparently, the only child of anthropologists. That Esther had married him at all had amazed us. We were born doubters, skeptics when it came to love. But who could ever account for taste? Just last year Suzie had run off with Emilio Saldariagga, leaving us behind for a polo field and a language she couldn't understand. True, Emilio had come to our town to train ponies, and few among us had not swooned at the height of his boots, at the way in which his hair, crow black, brushed the collar of his jacket. He was half her age, a gold digger, we knew, but Suzie never looked back, she said, until she returned, last month, with a woman named Carmen.

C'est la vie!

Esther ushered us in and shut the door, sweeping aside the sweep of her wrap to direct us to sit in a row.

"Walter wants to see your faces," she said, so we looked up to him and smiled.

Several of the candles were lined directly beneath Walter's portrait, their glow having the effect of turning him three-dimensional, expanding him, somehow: as if he understood the nature of the occasion—an *anniversary*, a *celebration*—and in no time he would make a wish and blow.

———

We have tried to be kind. Didn't we go along when Bambi organized the clothing drive? Who among us has not walked door-to-door to ask for nonperishables? Jell-o, Cup-a-Soup? But we are frugal by nature. Cautious. Suffice it to say we know the cold of these winters, the uncertainty of the market: Who can predict when canned cranberries might come in handy? When a rotted wool coat might be used for patching?

We have, in our lifetimes, known want.

———

The table was set with our covered dishes, still covered; Esther seemed to have forgotten all about them. She bustled around us, the dried flowers hanging by their stems, dandruffing her shoulders. She wore a muumuu of sorts, vaguely tropical, with embroidered neck and waist; a hand-me-down from her mother-in-law, perhaps, who had retired with Walter's father to New Guinea and lived comfortably among the cannibals. We had met her once at one of Esther and Walter's parties, a tiny woman named Sydney who sat in the corner scribbling. An artist, we had assumed, until she corrected us. Anthropologist, she said, showing us what she had written. We will never forget it: the look of our names in a stranger's hand, entered in a ledger. To help me remember, she said. What? Mimi Klondike had asked. All of this, she said, returning to her scribbling. Rudely, we would add.

Us? we thought. This?

We looked at what she meant. Esther's living room was filled with guests, though the house, as usual, appeared down at the heels. On the walls hung Esther's paintings, the earlier ones: portraits; still lifes that never looked quite still; then the more recent blazes of color—I adore orange! she'd say; fractured glass vases; an apple with a woman's face, or what suggested a woman's face, at its core. On her cherry side table, beneath a large canvas of the three Gorgons in blue unnaturally positioned around a birdbath, sat Esther's collection of porcelain Easter eggs. There would have been other things there—the carved whalebone and jade, the bird skeletons that Esther claimed inspired, the cloisonné cigarette box—but these had been cleared for the platter of ham, the basket of snowflake rolls, the horseradish. Beyond this, Lizzie Cooper and Katie Klondike, dressed in rented tuxedos, worked serving drinks from a makeshift wet bar, their faces bright red from the stolen dregs of our drinks; then the French doors through which we could see a slightly obscured view of Walter's tour de force, the goldenrod high and in bloom.

All of what? we said, turning back to Sydney, but she had disappeared.

Cocktail parties give her the hives, Esther told us later by way of explanation. She'd rather boogie-woogie with the natives.

We felt a lick, then, thinking of the natives, Goneril at our fingers, doggedly appreciative of the cheese from Barbara's antipasto. Esther stood at the head of us and suggested we begin, then disappeared again for fresh drinks. There were finger bowls at every place setting.

"Is this Japanese?" Mimi Klondike said.

"Chinese," we said.

Mimi shrugged. She put her tiny fingers into the finger bowl. "Chinese, Japanese," she said.

The candles burned their wicks, giving off a sweet odor, their shifting shadows against the fissured walls like so many black spiders in a web.

"I wonder why they never had children," Judy said. She was, she'd be the first to tell you, empty as a dried gourd. She'd tried for years and then abandoned ship to adopt Melissa.

"I used to stand at the screen door waiting for Megan to come home," Barbara said. "That's how much I missed her. And then when she'd walk in, I'd walk out. Anywhere. The Club. Anything."

"Most of the girls are having one now," said Viv.

"What?" Judy said.

"Or negative one. In Italy, I think, can you believe it? A place like that? I thought they always had a dozen."

"A dozen what?" said Judy.

"As far as I'm concerned, they've got the right idea," said Louise Cooper.

"They always have the right idea. Look at their salt and pepper shakers," said Mimi Klondike. "We were in San Giorno and I thought I'd died and gone to heaven. I told Mike I wanted to slip a few into my purse, that nobody would mind, that we were tourists, Americans. We were expected to behave badly. He said, 'Over my dead body.' Can you imagine? To salt and pepper shakers? Over my dead body, he said, and I told him. I really swore to him. That he was a pain in the ass and from that moment on I planned to travel on my own. If I got the notion, I told him, I might very well slip a Pietà into my suitcase and carry it through customs. Lord knows the British did. Never mind the Germans."

"The British?" Judy said. "What are we—"

"That was the beginning of the end," Mimi said. "I don't believe we spoke another word until Naples, when he had the nerve to hold up some godawful ashtray and say, How about this one, sweetheart?"

"I don't think Esther wanted them," Barbara said.

"What?" Viv said.

"Children."

"Children? Oh, Christ, children," Viv said.

Esther appeared in the doorway with fresh drinks on a tray. She set the tray down before us and dealt the glasses. Rings of water caught the candlelight and burned, magnifying the English hunting scenes on the coasters: horses that looked like so many Gonerils, bounding over green hills.

———

Suzie had caught on. What had been the beginning of the end? The dress shirts. "First the socks," she said. "Then the dress shirt buttoned at the wrists, then the necktie, then the dress shirt flaps tucked into the elastic of the boxer shorts. Then the trousers. I asked him one time if he couldn't possibly put on his trousers first. I said I would rather not witness a grown man walking around in blue boxer shorts, dress shirt, and tie. He looked at me as if I'd sprouted a second head."

We nodded, chewing. We had already agreed it impossible to detect Louise Cooper's cheese soufflé a Stouffer's, switched to her own ceramic pot. "I do it all the time," Louise said, mouth full, "no one's ever guessed."

"Charlie used to clear his throat," Barbara said. "Postnasal drip. Adenoids. Something like that. We were out to dinner, the Burts, and I asked him in the nicest of possible ways whether he could, for this one evening, stop making that sound."

The dessert plates were passed, the casseroles gone cold. The candles burned low in their wicks.

"Yes?" Judy said.

"That was ours," Barbara said, chewing. "The beginning of the end."

Esther, who ate nothing but sipped from the bowl of her drink, addressed Walter. "Did you hear that, sweetheart?" she said, as if a painting could be distracted, could be deep in its own thoughts, could have, just for an instant, lost the train of conversation. As it was, Walter didn't appear to miss a thing: We had never doubted his devotion to her—he carried it like a large wooden box, setting it by her feet wherever she paused. Now he stared down at us with his small, dark eyes, his homely mouth, bucktoothed, attempting to purse in the same disapproving expression. To either side of him hung black silk, intended for protection from the sun, to be drawn on particularly bright days, although the windows behind Esther were veined in ivy and faced north. We didn't need to look to know. Beneath him a row of stone elephants walked across the mantel toward an African drum, a twig of holly on its skin, and a series of glass jars housed shells, either minuscule or shattered, in what looked to be colored water—the entire mantel an altar to an alien spirit. It sat there with Walter in a room that was otherwise somewhat familiar: the Queen Anne dining chairs, the cherry table, the Oriental with its frayed fringe border, the pewter candelabrum. Even the cuckoo clock that flanked Walter's frame was the type that many of us kept in our foyers; if he had lifted a thin hand from his lap he might have reached out to still its pendulum, but he didn't budge.

We stared back, waiting for what to do next, his wife here at the head of us, wrapped in bleached cotton; how many years since his death? Six? Seven? Or had more time passed since we walked her to the grave, waited beneath that strange tent for the minister to close his book? She had collapsed then; she had wanted to climb in. How many could still remember holding her down?

We had guided her to the Club for chicken salad, which she ate, we noted. She would be fine, fine.

———

But she was not fine now; or was she? "Listen," Esther said, tapping the bowl of her drink. "I have brought you together for a reason." Here she looked around the table at each one of us. We looked back at her and the night beyond, the old Route 32, the shadows from the trees. There was a moon, strangely full and yellow. "You were my friends, weren't you?" Esther said. "I believed you were, though Walter said I trusted too easily." Here she shrugged. "Take anything. There isn't much, my doodles and some odds and ends; the cash is in the top drawer of our bedroom bureau. Walter hated banks.

"Oh, and answer any questions however you'd like."

She paused then and we squinted, waiting for her to go on. Questions? What questions did she mean? There were no longer any questions. She stood slowly and raised her chalice, directing her attention to Walter. The look of her hair! Could this truly be Esther? The one who wore the tiara to the Policemen's Ball? The rich girl who drove a white roadster, her red leather handbag bought to match its interior?

"I have always loved you," she said.

"I have never not loved you," she said.

"I will always love you," she said.

"Cheers!" Barbara said.

"Cheers!" Mimi said.

"What?" Judy said.

"We're toasting Esther's Walter," Canoe said, and there might have been tears in her eyes.

"Cheers!" Judy said.

"Cheers!" Louise said.

"Salut!" Viv said, because she would.

"Cheers!" Esther said, lifting the bowl of her drink higher. For a moment she looked as if she had just won a particularly difficult race and planned to douse herself with champagne, or gin, or whatever poison she held to her lips: a form of arsenic, we would later learn, a powder easily bought at the hardware store, intended for vermin. So like her to choose this way over waiting for the inevitable other, though we had not yet caught on. We live, ourselves, in a somewhat distracted state. Ethereal? No. Just removed from corporeal details. Still, we should have seen her flush in the shifting shadows, her determined stare over the lip of the silver bowl. She fixed her eyes on Walter as she drank, gulping as if there weren't time in the world to hit bottom. "Tonight, tonight," we heard Canoe say, perhaps in jest, perhaps not. We watched Esther only, transfixed, our fingers out for Goneril's thin, pink tongue. How long had it been since any of us were touched? Who among us could claim love?

And then suddenly we understood: Love. But what were we to do? We were nothing in the face of it. Onlookers, merely, the circle left behind.

Bambi Breaks for Freedom

———

It was absurd, really. He was probably already dead, and if not dead then he was old, which was worse. Still, Bambi stayed on hold, typically ignoring; it was past midnight. After a time she sat up straight. "Ivoryton, Connecticut," she said. "Jackson," she said. "Remington Jackson." She listened then wrote a number on a pad next to the telephone, the pen cap a whistle in her mouth. She spit it out and tapped it on the glass tabletop. *"Merci,"* she said, and hung up.

We waited, frankly concerned. Bambi had launched into another Break for Freedom, and though the previous ones had amounted to little—vaguely purple hair, an invitation, denied, to the UPS driver for a cocktail—this seemed more dangerous.

"He's there," she said.

"Where?" Judy wanted to know.

"For Christ's sake, Judy, we're talking about Renny—"

"I know."

"Jackson."

"I know."

Judy and Barbara stopped and turned to Bambi, who drew thin red hearts around the number.

"I adored him from the minute I saw him," Bambi said. "Pink oxford, frayed at the collar, with the most gorgeous curly hair. Not curly curly. Wavy. At the collar. Longish. This was 1945."

"You were eighteen years old," Barbara said, as if this meant something.

"He was from Maine of all places."

We nodded, or those of us still awake nodded. Canoe had stretched out on the wicker divan, her bunioned feet on one of Bambi's needlepoint pillows. Before her Breaks for Freedom, Bambi needlepointed: pillows, glass cases, footstools, tennis racquet covers. Who could blame her? There was not one among us who did not have a sample of Bambi's handiwork propped in the corner of our couch or holding open the door to the john.

"And green eyes."

"Charlie had green eyes," Barbara said, "which convinced me that Megan's would stay blue. They were this gorgeous pearly blue when she was born, and I wasn't the only one. Everyone said she'd keep them, even the doctor, and then, God knows, they went brown. It was overnight. Blue, brown."

"I'm calling," Bambi said.

"What time is it?" Judy said.

"Here I go," Bambi said. She popped the pen cap back on her finger and dialed, the bright light from the shell-encrusted desk lamp reflected like a dead exploding star in the window of the sunroom. Indeed, if we were to have looked out there, we would have seen nothing but our twin selves, suddenly old against the dense, black night.

———

The Breaks for Freedom began in January, in the weeks of the new year, the new century. Some drastic measures needed to be taken, Bambi said; something had to be done in a life: Esther dead, the Club temporarily closed for renovations. The first time she took the Greyhound to Manhattan, a sandwich in a paper bag and a knapsack stuffed with balls of yarn, debarking, she explained, at the Port Authority, the bus's pneumatic clutch released to expel her from the swinging door held open by a driver clearly schooled in cripples. These her words. She wheeled ahead, she said, through foul weather, crowded streets, the exhaust of Eighth Avenue. She had lived in Manhattan and knew as well as anyone the direction to the New York Public Library. She planned to eat her lunch in the glow of one of the green-glass lamps, read an early edition of Montaigne: the grand essayist! The master! French, originally. To assay. Did we know it? To make an attempt toward, to put to the test, to try.

Persevere, her father had said, parsing the word in his nightly prayer at her bedside, or as close as they would allow him to the iron lung. Polio. Her limbs, or at least three of them, petrified. Though it's a soft stone, she'd said. Chalk.

"You understand," she appealed to us; whom else did she have? "My need to occasionally flail."

Most of us had studied to be secretaries or teachers' aides—it was the highest we could reach: girls who substituted, who took dictation from war heros in gray suits. We enrolled in the colleges that specialized in this instruction, studying from the spiral-bound notebooks that covered what our teachers referred to as the three Gs: Grooming, Grammar, and Grace. Some of us dropped out before Grace, leaving after a first or second date, engaged; but some of us, the business types, were quite determined. We pictured ourselves ascending to Dow Chemical, our desks strategically placed outside the office of a man so important we would stand like a sentinel to his throne. This man never took on definite form; he was a cross between William Powell and Robert Mitchum. We were Barbara Stanwyck; we got things done. At the end of the day we slipped on our pumps and locked the office, our keys as heavy as doubloons in our Burberry pockets.

But Bambi. Bambi! Of her we knew this: In those years before the onset, hum a tune and she would sit down at any upright and play. Her gifts! The conservatory, the famous one, accepted her in a heartbeat. We met her at the Bachelors' Ball with Renny on her arm. We were newcomers, newlyweds; she a rumor in the town, a local legend, older than ourselves, a *professional*. The Two-Tones were performing, this before their tragedy, and at some point fireworks went off over the golf course. When she remembers him, she tells us, when she remembers that moment dancing—how he guided her, his cool hand against her back, his fingers dry as if powdered, weightless (he spun her out from their tips!)—it is in the spectacular light of the finale.

"Ringing," she said, her good hand cupped over the receiver, her bad arm, atrophied from elbow to wrist, propped on the pillow she had needlepointed soon after the diagnosis: Rosie the Riveter flexing her famously muscular arm, "We Can Do It!"

"What?" Judy wanted to know.

"She's calling Renny Jackson," Louise Cooper said.

"I thought he was dead," Judy said. "Isn't he dead?"

"He's in Ivoryton, Connecticut."

"Who told me he was dead?"

"Good evening," Bambi said, her voice steady, lower from the steroids she now took for pain. "I'm looking for Remington Jackson."

"What?" Judy said.

"Shut up!" Barbara said. We leaned forward in our chairs; Viv arrested at the wet bar.

"Yes, please," Bambi said, her voice grave. "It is somewhat of an emergency."

———

It was arranged. Saturday at four. He had taken a job in sales, and though he had long passed the mandatory retirement, they allowed him to call on a certain number of customers who had been particularly fond of him. It just so happened one of those customers was in our neck of the woods; he would kill two birds with one stone.

"He said that?" Suzie wanted to know. "Two birds with one stone? Our neck of the woods?"

"Something like that," Bambi said. "I was so nervous I could hardly hear him."

"Did he sound old?" Canoe said.

"This is Renny Jackson," Barbara said. "Remington Jackson."

"I'll see him on Saturday," Bambi said. "Saturday at four."

"I hope he still has hair," Canoe said. "I can't stand it when they're old and bald."

————

The day arrived as it will in our neck of the woods: stiff and cold, gray. We sat in the dim glow of Bambi's sunroom, plates of hard scrambled eggs on our laps. We would brunch! we had decided. We would think of what to say.

Bambi sat on her steel throne, a plaid car blanket tossed over her bone knees. She lit a cigarette and let the smoke dribble out the side of her mouth. "You really didn't know him well," she said, and we spoke not a word because *a:* She was right, we didn't know him well. How could we? We had simply danced, and *b:* These days Bambi rarely initiated any conversation. Barbara said, *depressed.* Clinically. Barbara knew the signs, had seen them in Megan. Not showering, Barbara had said. Silence, she had said. And then something about hair.

"We had plans to marry," Bambi continued. "Or rather, I wouldn't say plans, exactly. Plans is too specific, as if we had decided on, say, May second. We just had notions. We had talked. Made certain promises. And then, of course, our feet went numb." Here she smiled and lifted her bad arm with her good arm; we had grown accustomed to it: the cigarette crammed between the stiff fingers, the bad arm a utensil. Or this is how she described it: I'm limbs of steel, she'd say. I'm a kitchen drawer, she'd say.

"First mine, then his. In short order."

Canoe cleared her throat. "The one I wanted, I mean the one I should have had, was Alan Chapman," she said. She had her shoes off, though it must have been sixty degrees; she scratched one dry toe. "Buddy beat him to the punch."

"Alan Chapman is a raging alcoholic," Viv said.

"Why didn't you say no?" Louise Cooper said.

"What?" Canoe said.

"Why didn't you turn Buddy down?" Louise Cooper said.

"Are you nuts? And be an old maid?" Canoe looked around the room, but the rest of us paid little attention. We were waiting for Bambi; we had never known this about Renny, we had thought, been *told*, actually, that Bambi made the decision entirely herself, writing Renny a letter soon after the fever broke, her good hand guiding her bad hand, or this is how we envisioned it, the pen at an awkward, damaged angle, its line wavy, as if Bambi had not simply been struck down by illness but had aged fifty years as well. The letter said little, we understood. Simply that she had changed her mind, that she had decided she could no longer afford the lost practice time to romance, to ordinary pleasures—affection, family, et cetera—her gifts, she wrote, were what mattered. She had to think of her music.

I'd rather not engage in a long good-bye, she wrote, though we had found this exceptionally cruel.

Bambi stared back out at us through a wash of smoke.

"You really believed I'd give him up?"

The Two-Tones had quit early that night of the Bachelors' Ball, the thunderstorm appearing out of nowhere. We stood under the overhang at the Club looking out at the golf course, lightning cracking the sky as if the sky were a fragile, black thing: a black egg, black glass, black china. Something capable of being crunched, wrenched open; something entirely destructible.

"What if we're witnessing the end of the world?" Barbara said, or possibly Viv. We had all of us had too much to drink; the punch spiked, or one of us brought a flask. We huddled together as if for warmth, though a hot wind blew and we were bare-shouldered, our lollipop dresses sheathed in nothing more than chiffon stoles. We were beautiful then: newly married, not yet mothers. We smoked cigarettes and watched as the sky popped and fizzled, as clouds blew across the moon. Suffice it to say we were waiting for something, we didn't know what, reluctant to go home, reluctant to return to our husbands, preferring to stare out across the rolling night landscape, empty except for the shadowy trees in the rough. We must have sensed the two of them out there: how his breath fanned her neck, how the heat pressed down with a sweet and tangible weight, how they bucked and raced through that occasionally banished dark.

Now we stared at Bambi. Would she have given up Remington? We had believed it: she a bit older, a professional. If she had told us that on her first Break for Freedom she threw her wheelchair out the bus window and crawled to the New York Public Library, we would have pictured her clearly: *Christina's World* in Manhattan, the columns beckoning above the trees of Bryant Park, the passersby swerving to give her berth.

Perhaps she had never been to the library; perhaps she had simply ridden to the little airport on the outskirts of our town to watch the planes take off and land. This, we knew, she did from time to time. Mimi Klondike had spotted her in the Captain's Roost, her chair so close to the window the glass was fogged, Mimi said.

Bambi looked glazed, Mimi reported. Either drunk or happy. "If I have one wish before I die, my wish is just to fly and fly," she'd told Mimi.

"Is that someone I should have recognized?" Mimi wanted to know and of course Viv said, "The Scotsman, Burns." Then, "As in 'Should Auld Acquaintance be Forgot,'" but we paid little attention. We were picturing Bambi with her steel chair rolled to the glass, picturing her from the other side, the view the passengers would have had as they carefully picked their way down the small ladder that rose to the open airplane door. Windy, because the wind always blew there, and dark, their path outlined with tiny blue lights. They were in a hurry, of course. Who isn't? But if they had looked up before rushing to the airport entrance they might have noticed the woman above them, perhaps a woman, pressed to the window. And had they cared to stop they would surely have seen how her good hand pressed the glass in amphibian rage, the fingers splayed, gripping.

"The saddest ones, it could have been," Viv said.

"What?" Judy said; we had forgotten her in the corner.

"Another one. Burns. Of all the words of mice and—"

"Oh, for God's sake, Viv. Can it," Canoe says.

"'My love is like a red, red rose, / That's newly sprung in June; / O, my love is like a melody, / That's sweetly played in tune. / As fair art thou, my something something; / and I will love thee still.' Then something something something something, something something—"

Bambi has let the cigarette burn down in her bad hand. "He split," she says. "The minute he heard the diagnosis. Well, maybe he waited a morning, or a full day. I remember it as the minute."

She lowers her bad arm with her good, stubbing out the cigarette in a clamshell.

"We were children," she says.

"Dry!" Viv says. "Something something dry!"

———

Bambi was once, no contest, the best of us, her eyes huge and brown, doelike, her hair a shiny auburn. She had worn it pulled back from her face, some sort of ribbon tied around the band. And she'd been tall; we had forgotten.

———

Fury is part of it, Barbara told us. Rage. The sense, she said, of *helplessness*. These are the clues, she said, the Signs.

We thought of Megan, Barbara's daughter, in her senior year: Two hundred pounds and sullen, she seemed a walking advertisement, a sandwich board of Signs. We knew Megan was angry. Megan was helpless.

But Bambi? Shroud in wooly blankets, TV trays, a robe. She wore her hair shorn in the way of a survivor, easier to manage, she said, no brush. She might have been a spinster music teacher, though she no longer played. For a while she had tried, perfecting a kind of one-handed style, performing in small concert halls to sympathetic crowds. Hers became a novelty act, as shameful as Buffalo Bill's, she claimed, though to the rest of us it sounded grand: wheeled onto stage in a black gown, the lights lowered, her bad hand propped on a needlepointed pillow resembling piano keys in a joke no one could appreciate but her, her good arm raised to indicate the silence she needed in order to begin. And then, out of that silence, she would play, carving the music as if a sculptor with only a spoon for a tool. Scooping note to note.

Now she tapped her good hand, her *decent* fingers, she said, against the steel leg of her chair, impatient for Remington Jackson. Remington Jackson! Was he on his way? Would he soon arrive? None of us could answer, though we pictured him clearly: manicured, spritzed, a salesman ready to meet his next customer, whistling, a cross between William Powell and Robert Mitchum.

We scraped the dishes, stacked plates into the machine. We watered Bambi's dying plants and somewhere, someone vacuumed. If there had been brilliant sunlight it would have shone through her newly washed windows, but the gray had only deepened with the afternoon, exaggerating the streaks left by our rags.

A salesman! To think of him old now. Where had all the time gone? Wasn't it a summer evening, early July?

The cicadas were loud, we recalled. There would be rain; a thunderstorm of staggering proportions. The Two-Tones wore their signature tuxedos and red cummerbunds, the saxophonist's blue for reasons that seemed intentional, though we never learned. They stood in their four-man grouping on the flagstone patio of our Club, taking a break, smoking their cigarettes. This before the accident: the entire quartet wiped out in an instant, a jackknifed trailer in their path. Yet here, still, alive! There are things we will never not remember: the Bachelors' Ball, the beauty of our lollipop dresses and the rhinestones we begged to buy.

———

Barbara collects the plates and coffee cups, Bambi rolls from one room to the next. Judy suggests bridge, though none of us has the stomach for it. We play hearts until the squeak of Bambi's wheels ruins our concentration.

"Listen!" This from Bambi, her voice hoarse, newly ravaged. She looks in fever, her blanket thrown around her shoulders, her spindly, whittled legs bare. "I've got to get out!"

"What?"

"Please."

"It's quarter of four—" Canoe says.

Bambi's eyes blaze; she might be twenty-three, a beauty, a protégée. She might, at this moment, rise from her steel chair and stride across the room to where the piano, draped in a poncho, has stood unused for years. What song would she choose? "Slow Boat to China"?

"He tacked a letter to my door," she says. "He knew full well I was in the hospital. Everyone read it but me. *Sayonara*, it said. Yours truly."

"Give him the double jam," Canoe says.

"He said he had his career to consider. The awkwardness this would bring."

Louise Cooper grabs the handles of Bambi's steel chair, spinning her around so quickly the blanket draped on Bambi's shoulders drops to the floor and is caught beneath the wheels. Louise attempts to yank it out.

"Where are we going?" says Suzie.

"The Captain's Roost," Louise says.

"It's in the airport, off Route 32," Mimi Klondike says.

"We know," Barbara says.

"I'll get our coats," Canoe says.

"Hurry!" Bambi says, Louise still yanking. "Hurry! Hurry!"

What do we need? Our handbags. Our glasses. Our keys. Should we write our own note? Tack it to the front door? *Ciao, ciao*, we'd say. Tough luck, tootsie. But there's no time; in a minute we'll be caught, the headlights sharp. True, we're leaving signs of life: The house smells of egg and cigarettes;

the draperies pulled. But we can only do so much. We scurry to gather the coffee mugs, empty ashtrays. The planes are leaving, we know, their destinations announced over a loudspeaker.

"Are you sure?" Barbara asks.

"Hurry!" Bambi says, and we are suddenly aware that she can no more run than fly.

Louise frees the blanket, stumbling back a bit as Barbara grabs the handles and zooms Bambi to the ramp door, turning her around, leaning the door open as one might do at the Safeway with a particularly awkward handful.

"He broke my heart," Bambi says as Barbara steadies the chair, maneuvering it down the long, awkward ramp Bambi claims is a "Welcome" sign to criminals.

"He tore it right in two," she says.

———

The planes appear in the twilight: first stars. We have been here for hours, the ice in our cocktails melted down, our feet up on the badly upholstered bar chairs. We are the only customers; the bartender hiding from us in the kitchen, we believe, and the waitress long gone.

"At what point did your captain fly the roost?" Barbara had asked, and we all laughed, though the waitress only wiped her hands.

The lights get stronger and then the planes descend, small planes, twelve, twenty passengers at the most. They circle the airport, looping the clouds that at this moment have taken on a pearly sheen; it might be heaven, here. We eat fistfuls of nuts. We are famished. Earlier, there was talk of snow; the waitress said a northeaster had been predicted. We would sit it out, we told her. We would camp if need be, spend the night. She looked at us, tweezed eyebrows arched; she the type of woman we would never be: uniformed, large, her husband a retiree. And what did she think of us? Would she have guessed that we were schooled in the three Gs? That right now, swollen feet shoeless and propped on scratchy wool, one of us could recite the Scotsman, Burns? And another, the shorn-gray cripple parked in the corner, once played any tune by ear. Whistle something, we might have told the waitress, and she'll play like an angel. An absolute angel, we would say, because we always do. For emphasis.

"We're on a Break for Freedom," we told her. "On the lam from a man."

"Good for you, ladies," she said.

"We might never go home," we told her. She totaled the check and tore it off her pad, sliding it underneath our congested ashtray.

"Pay whenever you want," she said.

"We're never leaving," we said. "You'll have to sweep us off the floor."

"Good for you, ladies," she said.

"'As fair art thou, my bonnie lass, / So deep in love am I; / And I will love thee still, my dear, / Till all the something are dry,'" Viv says. "'And fair thee well, my only love. / And fair thee well a while. / Till something something something, love. / I'll hunt the crocodile.'"

She addresses a candle in a red-glass jar.

We are listening to her and then we are not; then we are again distracted by our view out the plate-glass window of the Captain's Roost to the brightly lit beyond. There planes putter down the short runway and brace for flight, their propellers sped to a whir.

Screw Martha

It was not our intention to end the day at a karaoke bar, but then we were adrift of intention. Wandering without a clue, as our daughters put it. And it felt warm here, besides. This Mustang Sally's, a place Suzie and Carmen had unearthed off Industrial Drive, a sliver of a bar sandwiched between an Empire Noodle and a Sheer Delight.

Earlier, we had strewn Barbara's daughter Megan's ashes into the reservoir off Memory Lane, once rutted and dirt but now paved with the asphalt that glitters in the dark. We were trespassing, of course, signs everywhere announcing the daylight hours we could have legally walked this road. Risking arrest, we resorted to stealth, an uncharacteristic urgency. The ashes had arrived weeks before by UPS, shipped to Barbara with a note from her ex, Charlie, that simply read, Our Megan. For a time she had kept them on her mantel, surrounded by baby pictures of Megan in silver frames, her unfortunate senior class portrait scowling from behind.

It is too cold for May, Memory Lane slippery with frost; soon bicyclists and joggers will overtake us, legal and peppy, but for now we are alone, hurrying single file, spruce branches brushing our arms, their pine smell so strong we might just lie down and doze, sleep into the next century. These were our woods—in the early years of our marriages, when we were pioneers—then we would come with the children, or alone. To leave the family sleeping wasn't yet a crime: the youngest in her crib; the boy in the top bunk. There were animals then, fox and beaver, occasionally a hawk, and a legend that something magical—a winged woman—lived in the wetlands.

Barbara walks at the head of our line, holding Megan in her urn. We do not need to see to picture Barbara: her face so similar to our own, framed in a short cut, balanced on a ribbed turtleneck. She wears small gold hoops purchased for their inconsequential shine and lipstick, a color from the seventies, something between pink and brown. The eyeliner she licked to draw has smudged in the slack, creased skin that fans her eyes, wrinkles she could not honestly attribute to laughter, or to a strong farm sun. Tennis, more likely. Or bourbon.

We reach a landing of sorts, what had once been a boat launch. A collection of boulders circles a patch of worn, purposeless grass stubbled with cigarette butts and pennies. In the center of the rocks a plaque reads that in 1776 the battle of S—— took place on these shores, resulting in the reencampment of Washington's troops to Paterson, New Jersey. Someone has written SCREW over the S——, and MARTHA over Washington. Canoe reads it aloud. "Screw Martha," she says. We wait for what else: Mimi Klondike claps her hands; Louise Cooper blows her nose. And the geese, on cue, skid out of nowhere to a crowd.

———

The day has dawned beautifully, a grayish mist rising from the reservoir. Carmen skips a stone. She landed here months ago, an exotic, off-course bird. Suzie brought her, though Carmen appears dazed, as if she might still be in the Southern Hemisphere—her pharmacy eyeshadow and large hoops. Chaps.

She tracks dirt. Smells of garlic and cigarettes. We've watched as she dumps packet after packet into her coffee, then dredges the sugar to eat with a spoon. She speaks with a lisp, new braces straightening her teeth; she could be forty-five or sixty, her hands mammoth. Suzie's told us she wakes every morning at four to run the curry comb over the haunches of Suzie's Morgan, to braid his mane and tail with red ribbon, to rub his hooves with flaxseed oil. As a little girl, Suzie's said, Carmen had no shoes and her father beat her raw. We know at one time there were rickets, crossed eyes, lice; we know too much, actually, and have asked Suzie to cool it.

Carmen skips another stone and we turn our backs, waiting for Barbara. What does she want us to do?

She untwists the urn and we peer in, remembering Megan as a little girl, not unlike any of our little girls—tights and patent leathers, a birthday party in July, balloons and streamers, barrettes, though Megan grew large and sullen, changing her name, as a teenager, to Gan. Here in the urn she is a pile of ash, not fine, as in cigarette, but rocky. Gravel, she, and we flesh and blood. "It's a terrible thing to outlive your child," Barbara says, as the geese rise and flap, furious.

———

We first encountered the flyer as an insert in the new monthly Club newsletter, then saw it posted outside the renovated Ladies' Locker, the wallpaper not of our taste though apparently there had been a vote.

The geese, the newsletter read, are a TREMENDOUS NUISANCE, a HEALTH HAZARD, DANGEROUS TO THE GENTLER SPECIES. Gentler species? Which? We were waiting for Pips Phelp, recently elected Club president, to explain. This at the gathering of Club associates, where Pips sat at the head of us in sweater vest and slacks.

"Friends," he said, though he was not our friend, Suzie the only one among us who had ever thought to visit his home, and this under duress. She'd gone to plead Carmen's case, wheeling Bambi along for cripple sympathy. "She came from nothing," she had told Pips. "She's a natural, a scratch handicap," Suzie had said—we heard it all from Bambi, who swore she didn't make a peep—a "regional paddle champion," Suzie said. "Excellent at doubles," she said. "A silver cup winner on the Argentine tour."

Pips gave them cold drinks in plastic cups; his wife,

Eleanor, and their bland children in Disney World. "We'll take it all under consideration," he said.

She could have rung Pips's wormy hands, Bambi said. She might have lunged from her wheelchair and rung his wormy hands. Suzie shifted her weight, grown substantial since Carmen, and her once-dyed hair she'd let evolve to gray. "I'm evolving in so many ways," she told us, hinting at sex, though we had already guessed.

"You'll have to propose her before the committee," Pips had told them. "What is she, a friend? A family member?" This said, according to Bambi, knowingly, Pips no fool, a closet millionaire, his new house of the Palladian style, impatiens within the circular drive, windows that held a sweeping view of the Brandywine. Suzie's color rose, Bambi said, but she pushed on, complimenting Pips on his collection of Revolutionary War battle maps. She had no idea he was a hobbyist! She'd love to see! He had walked them from 1776 clear through to 1783; the maps arranged chronologically, from the Battle of Germantown in the foyer to the surrender at Yorktown over the fireplace in the Great Room.

———

Pips had stood before the Club associates waiting for silence. "Listen up," he said. "Listen up." The minutes of the last closed meeting had already been read, along with a detailed accounting of the renovation. Now the names of the newly elected members were slowly and solemnly intoned by Jeannie Yeatman, our oldest living associate. She read the names in alphabetical order, pausing between each for either dramatic effect or to gulp another breath, her oxygen tank parked and at the ready behind. A familiar figure in the game room, Jeannie played bridge most mornings with a revolving group of biddies we called Them We Do Not Wish to Become, wizened gnomes, the humps on their backs like strange, bulky packages. She read the last name in her croaky voice then slowly folded the paper back into its neat square, passing it to Pips, who may or may not have looked, for a moment, toward Suzie, sitting dejected here among us.

"Mr. President," Jeannie Yeatman said. "Proceed with the meeting."

The last sentence took its toll. Jeannie stumbled backward and reached for the arm of her chair, thankfully one of the floral upholstered brought from the Ladies' Locker expressly for this purpose. Betty Dugan, Club secretary, reconnected her, and the whir of Jeannie's oxygen machine temporarily cut off Pips, who waited, again, for everyone to settle.

"We are in the center of a noose," he began, and you could have heard a pin drop. Yes, it was the same Pips who had played Him in our Intervention, however dull, however miscast from our point of view, a poor substitute, a Her-Him, Mimi had said, and we had each given her five. The same Pips who had often stood before us, his waistband elastic, his shoes of a white and recently shined leather. But now he seemed a different Pips, a man who might have held within his frame the shadow of a younger man, a soldier who had launched battles on the shores of faraway lands, a man who raised a scepter and led the way. The whole room gathered its breath, waiting, the only sound that of the whir of Jeannie's oxygen.

"A noose of convenience, *noto bene*? A trip to the casino, a new pair of sneakers, a Discman." We saw the Discman before us like chewed gristle, and waited, uncomprehending; although we trusted Pips would soon make sense, the fact that he had actually spoken the word *Discman* during a Club associates meeting in a room that would later be used for cotillion slightly thrilled us, and we hoped for something dangerous.

"It's the Mall at Governor's Picnic, the Mall at Sea-Cliff Manor, the Mall at Teddy's Turnabout, the Mall at River Run. It's Brandywine Dales, Brandywine Hills, Brandywine Crossing, Brandywine Forged." We saw, now, that Pips read from a prepared text.

"Strangers circle us, driving their vans around and around what has become our tiny green oasis, shopping, shopping, shopping, crowding in all the detritus of their lives onto our own: the filth, the trash, the *geese*."

A small, inconsequential voice from the back said, "Geese?"

"I will pass around a sign-up sheet. We will take them on in groups of five. I will tell you this is only the beginning. I will tell you that it will be a long battle, replete with victories and losses. But it's a battle for our selves, our way of life: its fairways and greens. What many of us hold to be self-evident, but which now requires defending.

"With your help they will be netted and then, in conjunction with the Department of Health and the Animal Welfare people, exterminated. In the meantime, we coat their eggs with oil."

The small, inconsequential voice said, "Oil?"

"Questions?" Pips said, a challenge.

Suzie raised her hand.

"Good," Pips said. "The instructions are made clear in the flyers Betty will now pass around. They will be posted as well later this week on the minutes board. In short, we need your help. Whenever apprehending a nest of eggs, please alert Club officials to the location so we can oil them." Pips cleared his throat. "For your edification," he said, "oil prevents the passage of oxygen through the eggshell, thus asphyxiating the gosling."

"Oil as a verb?" Canoe said. "This is bullshit."

"Good," Pips said. "Any questions?"

Suzie raised her hand.

"Bullshit fairways and greens," Canoe said. "Bullshit our way of life."

"Good," Pips said. "Adjourned."

———

It was Carmen who found the nest, not so long after Pips's call to arms. She had been illegally riding Suzie's Morgan near the reservoir, Memory Lane no longer open to animals of any kind—we used to run our dogs here when our dogs were still alive—though a trail had recently been forged near the fence; it circled the reservoir then ascended Bishop's

Hill, once a sledding hill, we remembered, before Elizabeth Stilton's accident and the adoption of the Toboggan Law.

We explained it all to Carmen. Heapfuls of snow—accumulations in feet not inches—and past winter days of sun and blue skies, snowsuits, mittened children on newly waxed sleds. We served hot chocolate with marshmallows. We made sandwiches. Our hair was longer then and our teeth white and we did not stop to consider anything but warming frozen fingers and what to thaw for dinner, a drink at six enough of something to look forward to, a clean house enormously pleasing.

Or was it all, as our daughters like to remind us, excruciating?

Huge, Carmen continues. She makes a circle with her arms. *Stupendous*, she lisps. She's in the middle of us, sitting in chaps and boots beneath a rack of hanging copper pots at Suzie's kitchen table, her hard hat on the table. The mud she tracks, we think; she is never without a trail.

She tilts the hard hat to show us the egg, partially wrapped in what looks to be a baby's knitted cap. It is a giant of an egg, a yellowish globe. We stare at its mud-splattered shell as if at a globe: California, Argentina. Florida, where word has recently come that Megan hanged herself in the garden shed of Charlie's beach house, no note of explanation, no warning, simply a girl whom we knew as a baby, dead.

Barbara appears fine. She sits opposite Carmen at the head of the table, dressed in a light checked jacket and slacks, her legs crossed, her arms folded listening to Suzie's translation of Carmen's story. Apparently Carmen had gone out before dawn to ride the new reservoir trail. She found the nest near the point where it turned up Bishop's Hill.

"Stupendous, no?" Carmen lisps, again.

Carmen looks from the hard hat to Suzie, something unspoken passing between them.

"It's sad, actually," Suzie says.

"It's all sad," says Bambi, parked beyond us.

"I'd like to hold it," Barbara says; this from her place at the head of the table. The sound of her voice startles us, and it is only then that we realize she has not yet spoken. Still, we wish her silent a bit longer; we'd like more time to pass; to return to our green oasis, to the girls in their snowsuits, mittens clipped to pink sleeves, cold tears on their wind-burned cheeks. We can still see them perfectly, piled like so many dominoes on the sleek board of the toboggan, poised at the top of the hill. They are good girls; they wait for us to give the word before heading down.

Barbara reaches across to Carmen, who lifts the egg, slipping it from its wooly hat.

"It's probably already dead," Barbara says, holding it to her ear. She listens as if hearing.

Canoe squeaks, "It's bloody hot in here."

"Last count three hundred and twenty-six," Mimi Klondike says.

"What?" Bambi says.

"I can't *breathe*," Canoe says.

"Three hundred and twenty-six oiled and returned to their nests," Mimi Klondike says. "Front page of the newsletter."

"What's the point of returning them to their nest?"
Bambi says.

"Something to do with instinct. Recasting the maternal
instinct," Mimi Klondike says. "I read it."

"I didn't get that one," Judy says. "Was that April's?"

"Hah! Maternal instinct," Bambi says. "Toss her to me,
darling."

Barbara pitches and we watch as the egg sails through
the air.

"Look, Ma, I'm flyin'!" squeaks Canoe as Bambi catches
it, tossing the egg high again. "Weightless," she says. "And
empty." She brings the egg down hard against the padded
arm of her wheelchair, the crack not that of lightning or a
gun, but of a stick inconsequentially snapped.

What next?

In fairy tales the gosling tumbles out, formed to perfec-
tion, shaking its white, downy feathers, slowly unfolding its
wings. First one shaky step, then two, as it lifts off Suzie's
kitchen floor, veering toward the kitchen window out. We
watch proudly as it soars away. Look what it has learned in
our careful care! Nature? Nurture! See how it negotiates
the wind's currents, banks our gravel drives and crumbling
stone walls, our fields of barking dogs, our abandoned play-
grounds and once sleek horses, our rusting automobiles and
mulched gardens and roads and roads and roads, ascending
like the fabled crane through the clouds to disappear

heavenward, hell-bent on adventure, on reaching the king-
dom of the gods.

But the egg is empty. Dust.

———

Bambi said she knew as much, knew it too light to hold anything. It's late in the evening at Mustang Sally's, long after
the colored lights lit us up onstage to sing "Sweet Caroline,"
an encore to Carmen's "Volare." Italian, Spanish, she seemed
to know it all, but what had Suzie just told us? Saved by the
Jesuits? Educated in Paris?

"She rose from nothing," Suzie says. "It's an outrage she
was blackballed.""

"Hear, hear!" says Viv.

"Stupendous!" Bambi says.

We raise our glasses, the pulse of the amplified bass as
insistent as our own.

"Screw Martha!" Canoe says, and we clink.

———

But first, earlier, Barbara asks us all to help, to please pick a
piece of Megan to toss out to the reservoir. Megan would
have appreciated that, she says. She says that in the end
Megan didn't like her much, but she thinks Megan would
have loved the look of so many women here to scatter her
ashes across the water. Maybe Megan is watching and listening right now, she says, maybe her Megan is somewhere here

among us right this minute, not in this urn but somewhere else. She says, Maybe all of them are, watching—and by them we are not sure whether she means the dead, or the living, though it seems monumental, this invocation. Historical in a way we'll never be.

———

The geese return, swooping, honking, formed in a perfect V; they survive on the outskirts, their strength in numbers. In time, perhaps, their flocks will dwindle—they are pursued!— but on this morning they don't give a damn.

Barbara cries and we let her. We are not cruel, understand. Nor are we anything other than who our daughters will become. But we wish it over, this display; we'd like it gone. Because there's nothing to be done, we could tell them; because death comes to all the living; because they think us heartless and we are, somewhat, our hearts worn down by the slow drumming of our blood.

Come As You Were

We were married in white dresses, our husbands-to-be spit-polished at the end of the aisle. It happened too quickly. This explains the party, or in Canoe's mind, should have explained the party: Come as you were, she said. No use having them sit on mothballs.

Canoe is newly wagon-free. I've not fallen, I've leapt, is what she says. Plunged. Lurched. I dived, she says, or is it dove?

"Dived," Viv says. "Like hanged and hung."

"That's what Charlie said when he called about Megan," Barbara says. "It was all I could do not to correct him. I mean, that was my first thought. It's hanged, I wanted to say. *Hanged.*"

This a garden party, steamy June, the date chosen for the fact of its length, the solstice. In Scandinavia the sun will not set and if there we would eat a meal of salmon and black bread at 3:30 A.M., play tennis at 4:00; in the jungles of Mexico crowds gather around the base of the pyramids, waiting for the sun to hit the precise right angle to cast the shadow serpent who devours stone.

Here it is simply the longest day. We form a tiny circle, there are no other guests. Past parties, there were many. We would look out over Canoe's mowed fields and just beyond to the pasture where her daughter Anne kept a horse; it often waited there, just at the edge of us, its speckled muzzle, dark eyes.

Who knows what waits in that field now? The trees have grown into a wood, the pasture left to seed. Within the rows of daylilies snakes ivy, poison and otherwise; you wouldn't want to pick them. Packs of browned daffodils, browned iris, sprout from various beds, irrational, Canoe's interest elsewhere. In the moon garden she has planted foxglove, dianthus, a surprising number of petunias, though she once swore she wouldn't be caught dead. The garden glows at the far edge of the property. She can see it from her widow's walk, she says, where she waits for the return of her men.

Before there were suitors, and gardeners, too; but Ricardo hasn't got the time, he explained to her earlier, given the responsibility of the pool.

"Can him," Louise Cooper says. "Give him his walking papers."

"Oh, Christ," says Canoe. "Then what?"

Louise Cooper shrugs. "Hire another?"

We all laugh and turn to the newly arrived Suzie, Carmen in tow like a tamed pet. She is wrapped in Suzie's train, longer and certainly more expensive than any of ours: yards of Belgian lace. Carmen slowly unravels, her fingernails, we would worry, too long not to snag some of the delicate handiwork, though Suzie couldn't care less: She's a DuPont some generations and wears her money lightly—a casual Jaguar, casual Coach bags, Ferragamos. Now this, what we all imagine we wanted, a gown of tulle and Belgian lace, mother-of-pearl buttons up either sleeve, a sweetheart collar, and one double-wide, moss-green ribbon stitched on either side seam. "Carmen's idea," she says. "I would have popped right out."

Nursie sewed it all by hand, Suzie tells us. She had stood for the fittings on two pillows pulled from her mum's bed. Nursie sewed around her, pins in her mouth. "I can still picture her there, hair in a bun, shoulders hunched. She was the kindest little woman. This button was my something old, worn by her on her own wedding day, though God knows what happened to the husband."

"Had sewn," Viv says.

"What?" says Suzie.

"Oh, for Christ's sakes, Viv," Canoe says.

Carmen twirls back into the train and follows after Suzie, a chrysalis and a butterfly. They break the dusk, fireflies sparking their path. You could spoon this heat, eat a bowl of it. We should have convinced Canoe to move the party to October, though she said nonsense. Weren't we all June brides? And it was true. Each one of us.

Suzie and Carmen descend the stone steps to the swimming pool, where candles float on scallop shells and Ricardo waits in tails. He is no doubt flummoxed by his employer, who until this evening had insisted that no matter how sweetly she asked, she was not to be permitted a drop.

"Hah, hah!" she said earlier, rattling her ice under his nose. "Ri-CAR-dough," she called. "Hah!"

"Stunning," Gay Burt says of Bambi, who rolls up in concert black and sequins, a boa around her shoulders. "Think of me as the groom," Bambi says. We nod, though we are distracted by Ricardo, who has just whipped off his tails and dress shirt. "Hah, hah!" he's saying as Suzie and Carmen applaud. We have never seen anything quite like him, Ricardo. He lives on the other side of the Grange in one of the trailers in the trailer park that has been there for generations. Canoe says he just wandered up one night, knocked on her living room window while she watched some program. What was she to do? Send him back from whence he came?

"He's been so *kind* to me," she says.

We guide her down the stone steps toward a chaise longue, Carmen and Suzie making her a plate with one of the sandwiches Ricardo earlier ordered from the Gilded Goose— sun-dried tomatoes, goat cheese, black olives. "Here," Carmen urges. "Here, baby."

Canoe nods, loopy. We should never have let her get this way, but she's our hostess, so who's to argue? We think of her fortieth, how Buddy decorated her as she lay snoring on the couch. The party had been a surprise, the only clue the black balloons that lined the drive and the children mysteriously absent, packed off to the neighbors just after lunch. The theme had been our lost twenties, and the last time we had seen Canoe upright she had been hula-hooping, gloves to her elbows, a cigarette holder scissored between two satin fingers. Buddy drew a red mustache and pitched red eyebrows, devilish, on her slack face, the lipstick a shade we recognized from our own handbags; he powdered her hair gray, wrapped her legs in black crepe. In Anne's room he found stuffed animals, the farm kind, pigs and horses and a spineless cow. He balanced several on Canoe's shoulders, flopped the cow on her head—as if she were a drugged Gulliver, tied down by Lilliputians—the effect somewhat comical. Well, the men laughed and so did we and then Buddy, no doubt bolstered, wrote Kick Me across the bare, freckled skin of Canoe's chest and signed it with what we recognized from our own notes, from the commands we left around the house: ☺.

Someone had a Polaroid, and in the photograph Canoe remains dead to the world, all of us and some of our husbands crowded around her, our faces bright. She framed it in a five-and-dime frame and hung it just over the powder room john—History preserves my finest moment, she said; The pinnacle of me—though the Polaroid bleached out, as they will, and in no time we all could have been anyone.

Up the slope Gay Burt now keeps Bambi company, Bambi's wheelchair too difficult to negotiate down. She has come in full regalia, Gay—her gown an organdy satin, boat neck with tiny, beautifully pressed pleats to a cinched waist. This is good for her, Barbara says. She's seen the signs, she says. She thinks Gay might need some professional guidance, she says. Imagine waking up with half a nose, she says, it's like something out of a bad dream. We look toward Gay, the dusk deepening so that Gay looks disappeared within her white, fireflies flashing from time to time as phosphorescence would on a dark sea. It feels like a dark sea, the heat not solid after all, but something you could drown in. We picture her going down, Gay Burt, her wedding dress billowing, the skirt a perfect, white circle, a bull's eye in which her nose, or what's left of it, is the center, a nose that's been repaired, patched—with what? Her elbow? Her hip? The flesh from her buttocks? They took it from all parts, she said; they wanted to test what would stick. We try not to stare though it's difficult; quilted, she looks. Go ahead, she's said to us, smiling. *Admire me.*

———

We were all once lighthearted. Virgins, or once or twice removed. We didn't know a thing. Go on, we say to Gay. This much later, after Gay has been persuaded to join us near the pool, Bambi carried down the stone steps in the cradle of Carmen's rock-hard arms. (Do we have any idea of their strength? Suzie tells us. The muscle needed to reign in those Morgans?)

It's cooler here, and there's lavender planted nearby; even with no breeze we can smell it. The time must be close to ten, and though you could no longer call it dusk, there are shades of red on the horizon, or what once was the horizon. The new woods crowd our view. We are ringed by trees, by the rising cicada hum, or is it a buzz? Still, beyond where Anne's horse once stood—bored, flatulent, pathetic in its weak neighs—the sun has not entirely set.

We sit on wrought iron or on the hard flagstone that borders the pool; someone balances at Canoe's feet. She lies splayed on the chaise, lightly snoring. We have eaten the cold pasta salad, the salmon, the sandwiches of goat cheese and olives, of sun-dried tomatoes; our cocktail napkins read "Who Invited All These Tacky People?" Beyond our circle we see the glow of Ricardo's cigarette.

Go on, we say to Gay Burt.

Gay gathers some volume of skirt in her hands, her fingernails, we know without a closer look, painted in the French manner, her hands delicate. It is only recently that Gay Burt has chosen our company. We've always known who she *was*—ex-wife to Clark Burt, an unmitigated bore and frankly, we suspected, homosexual. We'd see her with her sister, Katherine, a poet who apparently suffered migraines. Katherine had moved to our town soon after Gay Burt divorced Clark, and though Gay Burt had always struck us as the independent sort, she seemed completely devoted to Katherine, chauffeuring her to the various Municipal Arts events, to the Winter Fair at Briarcliff, even courtside at the TenniTour, though we could no more imagine Katherine's interest in tennis than the man in the moon's! Katherine's death had not shocked us—she seemed ill even on the brightest of days—but Gay's sudden attention came as a surprise. She'd always stayed apart. Perfectly polite; we'd known her for years: Hadn't she come from a desperately poor family in Queens? Or was that Amanda Burkas? The point is, Gay appeared one morning fresh from surgery. The usual. Sunspots, malignant. She'd seen Dr. F, who has done Viv's chin, Barbara's eyes, Bambi's varicose veins, and so we assured her that nose or no nose, she was in the right hands. "I need a drink," is what she had said that morning. We were at Viv's eating huevos rancheros. "Have I come to the right locale?"

―――――

I hid in the armoire and wept, Gay begins. (What she needs is *friends*, Barbara had said after Gay'd left Viv's that day. And we had seen the word *friends* as a pebble tossed into a pond, the rings it cast expanding wider and wider—*friends!*— though the rings encompassed nothing but a sheen of light, a reflection disturbed by breeze or the flutter of a dragonfly's wings. We were company, perhaps; women of a certain age with shared interests. But friends? It seemed too intimate, somehow, wrong.) Clark assumed I'd gone to the john, Gay continued.

I watched him through a crack in the door. It was an old hotel in the historic district. Cape May, she says.

We stay quiet, thinking. We have our own stories, don't we?

The woman who owned the place had led them up the stairs, Gay said, Clark insisting on carrying the suitcases though the woman's son was perfectly able, sulking by the front desk, leering at them as if he could picture the rest of the night. The woman didn't stop talking; she asked about the wedding, about the number of guests, about the flower arrangements, the food. Clark struggled behind with the suitcases—they were on the fifth floor, the wedding suite with a view of the Atlantic, or at least the possibility of smelling the ocean if the wind was right. The woman opened the windows and said, "There," as if the breeze were enough, the night air.

"Good night," she said, and Gay wanted to grab her hand, to say she hadn't yet told her about the reception, about the toasts, the lovely one made by Katherine, who just that spring had been accepted to Radcliffe and planned on never marrying and writing books and thought that Gay was out of her mind, yes, out of her mind, is how Katherine put it; reconsider, she had said. We'll set up house like Virginia and Vanessa.

"Who?" Mimi Klondike says.

The idea of that was *impossible*. Impossible, she wanted to tell the hotelwoman, whose big bosom still heaved from climbing the stairs. It seemed impossible not to marry, *impossible*, but the hotelwoman was already saying good night, saying breakfast could be served anytime so don't worry about waking early, saying, See? Smell that sea?

Then she was gone and Clark remained, unpacking his things into the bureau in the other room. She could take the armoire, he called, and so she did, curling up into a tight knot, closing the door as best she could. Some time passed before she heard Clark enter the room. He wore pajamas—she could barely see from there—and slippers of some sort, and he sat on the edge of the bed, his hands between his knees. "Gay?" he said after a time, but she did not answer. She tucked her knees up, made herself smaller than she already was; she thought of her father giving his toast, pleased, no doubt, to be the center of attention, his ears pink. "I'm none too happy to pass Gay on to such an extraordinary gentleman," he had said.

Suddenly Clark was there in the armoire doorway, his pajamas striped.

"Gay?" he said.

"Yes?" she said.

"Are you sick?"

"I'm fine."

He stood there for a moment; she uncurled a bit. She still wore her pink traveling dress, ordered from Bonwit's; her matching pillbox hat sat on one of the pillows on the bed, huge from here, smack in the center of the room.

"Do you need help getting out?" Clark said. She had placed one foot on the floor and was pushing up with both hands.

"I can do it," she said.

"Great," he said.

She was sixteen years old; she was twenty-two; she was fifty-three. It didn't matter; she didn't know a thing.

"I can do it," she said.

He put his arm out to steady her and she took it, feeling oddly kind toward him. "I feel like a lorgnette," she said.

"A what?"

She looked at him. She had met him six months ago at a dance. He had been to school in the South and now worked in his father's garment business in Indianapolis; they had danced to "Be My Love," to "Too Young." The dance had been at the resort on Mackinaw Island where she worked clearing glasses and plates from the large round tables in the formal dining room, windows looking out to the lake. There on certain days water-skiers were pulled crisscross and you could, if the windows were propped open, hear their screams. She would never have been able to afford coming here as a guest, but her sister had befriended one of the restaurant managers, and the two were given jobs and bunks in the employee cabin. They had separate shifts, since the manager quickly saw it was near to impossible to have them work together; Katherine would pull Gay aside and point at one of the ancient diners, men and women who smelled of baby powder and cologne. "War hero," Katherine would say. "Kraut spy," she would say. "Stalin lover."

"An opera glass," Gay said to Clark. "One of those glasses to look through."

"You've got one?" he said.

"Never mind," she said.

He had been a guest at the resort, a day visitor persuaded to stay for the dance. A Kraut spy's grandson, immediately and entirely dismissed by Katherine, who said that his ears were far too large and that his chin showed signs of multiplying in the imminent future.

Or is it eminent? she said; she took a long drag on her cigarette and crossed her legs. Her waitress uniform hitched high above her knees, though she refused the required slip.

"Imminent," Gay said, crossing her own legs.

"You say potato," she said, and smiled. "Besides," she said, "he's from Indianapolis."

"We're from Queens," Gay said.

"Exactly," said Katherine. "You're supposed to move up the food chain; it's natural law. Darwin. Evolution."

"I think he's cute," Gay said.

"Consider the children," Katherine said. "Do you want children from the Midwest?"

Gay reached over and scissored the air. Katherine passed her cigarette and stood up.

"I'm late," she said.

"Good-bye," Gay said.

"Don't do anything foolish," Katherine said. She looked at Gay then in a way Gay would always remember; it was as if Katherine were leaving for more than her shift, as if she were, in fact, planning on going back to their cabin and packing her bags, disappearing into the woods that bordered this lake to live out her days in the hollow of a tree. Foreign, Gay might have said. A foreign look, or better, a distant one. Something had at that moment cleaved them.

"Gay?" Clark said.

"I'm here," she said, looking up. His ears were, in fact, quite round, or perhaps they only looked round now, with his new haircut and here, standing here, in his striped pajamas and slippers. She had never seen him in pajamas.

She smiled and he began to kiss her, first her lips, which she liked and knew the feel of, and then her neck. His hands moved to the zipper there and he slowly unzipped her dress, kissing her lips, again, as if his hands were only accidentally slipping the dress off her shoulders, tugging it to drop around her ankles, which it did. She still wore her heels and worried, for a moment, that she might stumble if she tried to move, the dress wrapped around her ankles now, spiked by heels higher than she was accustomed to, her mother insisting that she buy proper women's shoes rather than the sandals Gay had wanted. She thought of this and other things: the douche in her trousseau, presented by Katherine the night before. Whatever you do, Katherine had said, don't get knocked up the first time. The negligee her mother had ordered with the pink traveling dress from Bonwit's, how her mother had unwrapped it from the tissue paper and held it up against the window light. "It's called sheer ecstasy," her mother had said. Gay had looked at her mother then, a thin woman who in the sharp light appeared as sheer as the negligee; her mother looked back and shrugged. "Don't ask me," she said.

Gay feels a sinking, hollow feeling; somehow she stands in nothing more than brassiere, underwear, and high heels in a room in a town where she has never been that smells no more like the sea than the room she shared with Katherine in Queens. Where did Katherine go? To the hollowed-out tree? For a swim in the lake? No doubt right now, this late, Katherine read in bed, the Smith-Corona she won as vale-dictorian sitting on the kitchen table, a stack of white paper beside it at the ready; if she were there, she might lie down next to her, she might even lean against her shoulder and ask if Katherine could please, just this once, read to her, lov-ing nothing more than the sound of words in her sister's voice.

Clark has unbuttoned his pajama top and Gay stares now at the hair that curls around his nipples. It is not that she is afraid of this, exactly, of what will eventually come to pass— she has thought of it often, pictured it as best she could, from books, mostly, and a few conversations with Katherine. She has even wanted it, with other boys mostly; after dances, dates, when she would linger in the shadow of a car, within or without, pressed into a boy, her back arched to get closer, aware of his hands on her skin, of the feel of his fingers almost to the point she wills them to find before saying stop. Yet somehow, here with the boy she has married, she feels numb. Perhaps it is his expectation, indeed the expectation of all of them of what this night will bring. It turns her stomach, makes her want to lie down and sleep. Or perhaps it is nothing more than a dark mole she has just noticed imbedded within the hair on his chest.

"Excuse me," she says.

She steps out of her high heels, out of the dress around her ankles; he is not a criminal. This he will say the next night, and the next. "I am not a criminal," he will say. "This is legal, Gay," he will say, articulating her name in the way one does the name of a child, or a particularly deaf relative when summoning patience.

She will shake her head, attempt a smile. Fiddle-dee-dee, she might say, though some nights she says nothing at all, simply walks into the bathroom and locks the door.

A silence settles in—no one sure whether Gay has finished her story, or whether there's more. Of course there's more; the question is whether she plans to tell it. But Gay appears to be drifting, her dress still caught in her hand.

"He called me frigid," she says at last. "I had to look it up."

They are stupendous, these fireflies: a rash of them. The heat brings them on, and the sweet, sticky smell of buddleia.

"I thought you prayed to God," Viv says. "Don said he'd never seen anything like me. A college graduate. *Summa cum laude.* He said I was one in a million, an idiot, he said, but it's true, I swear to you, I thought you went to church and kneeled and prayed."

"Then what?" Barbara says.

Viv shrugs. "Something happened?"

We all feel a certain tension in the dark, in the languid white moths that rise and fall within the moon garden, in the sudden, gushing sound of the pump filtering Canoe's pool water. There's heat here; the threat of rain.

"I never had one," Mimi Klondike says.

"What?" Barbara says.

"You know," Mimi Klondike says.

Bambi rolls her wheelchair back and forth irritably; Louise Cooper folds her napkin into an accordion fan. She, of all of us, might have something to add, but she stays quiet. Somewhere a thundercloud descends, or rises; storms just as easily assembled by uncontained fires; we've read about this—the funnels certain fires can bring on, the whoosh of it, the rush; at any moment we might be drenched.

"Mike said it was entirely in my mind. He said I chose not

to enjoy myself," Mimi Klondike says. "I said, perhaps you're just lousy at it, whatever the hell 'it' was. I had nothing to compare him to, so I just grinned and bore it. Sometimes I squeaked a little to amuse myself. I had all sorts of games I'd play."

Carmen and Suzie look on, holding hands, the veil a blanket wrapped around them despite the heat.

"I made up a lover once," Barbara says. She would be the one to say it—given her recent therapy, her conversion, as she puts it, to honest living. She would be the one to breathe the word *lover*, as if it were a word that any of us might drop into a conversation, or even suggest. *Lover* is not a word in our lives, nor in the lives of anyone we know: It's too animal, somehow; too raw. It suggests dime-store novels and intrigue, everything impractical. Still, there's a little trill to the word when she says it, as if a hovering fairy has just rung a tiny brass bell. Who among us has not wished for that? The lover who doesn't say a thing, who slips between the sheets. He kneads our legs with his toes—we should have remembered to shave!—kisses our neck, pushes his tongue into our ear. He laps us up, swallows us—we are nothing solid at all, we could tell Gay Burt. We never were! No suitcase, no needlepoint, no lorgnette; nothing! All this effort, and see? We are only fishy water, something to be drunk down in one draw or, better, evaporated into air on a night as hot as this one.

"I called him Ted," Barbara says. "I told Charlie I'd known him in high school, though we'd just been friends. I told Charlie he'd made a fortune in some pharmaceutical, that he'd just lost his wife, that I had intended to simply offer condolences, but that one thing had led to another."

"What?" Canoe says. She hitches herself up on one of the plaid pillows we have brought from the pool house. "What are we talking about?"

"Sex," Barbara says.

Canoe leans back, laughing, hers a simple white poplin with square bosom and sleeves of eyelet lace.

"Sex?" she says. "I'd rather pull weeds."

———

Later Canoe sips coffee, dunking one of the lace cookies brought by Barbara. She's in the middle of it.

"Mother claimed she saw him ride down the Mall toward the White House, or maybe it was the Capitol, nearly every morning. Apparently he rode an Arabian, its name known to everyone in Washington. Anyway, one day he saw her watching him from the window and waved to her and she waved back and after that he would always wave (this Teddy Roosevelt) until one day—and Mother swore to it on her father's grave—he called to her to come down and he lifted her to the back of the horse—nobody used saddles then— and was about to whisk her off for a ride when my grand-mother Nettle opened the door with her yellow sash and said, Excuse me, Mr. President, but if my daughter is going to go galavanting about the town with you, I would like her to be properly dressed. By that she meant the yellow sash, of course. She was a furious suffragette.

"They lived in Georgetown. Very very. She was an only child. Her father adored her and so on and so on. She made a bad match, that's what Grandmother Nettle used to tell me: Your mother's made a bad match.

"Sonofabitch," Canoe says.

"Teddy Roosevelt?" Barbara says. She lost Canoe back at the yellow sash.

Canoe drains her coffee. "Him, too," she says.

"What happened?" Suzie says.

Canoe looks from one to the next; when did she get so old? When did she find herself surrounded by women?

"He refused to take her. Lifted her back off the horse and tipped his hat at Grandmother Nettle, rode old what's-his-name into the sunset. Apparently Grandmother Nettle gave him the bird; she said hers was the last great generation. Of women, that is. She used to tell Mother that the rest of them, of us, had gone straight downhill. Disappointing to the whole lot. Et cetera, et cetera. Mother couldn't have cared less. It was Teddy she loved. She said the day that he died was just horrible for her. She lined up with the rest of the hordes to watch him pass in state. Beautiful, a blanket of purple velvet across his casket and that horse of his slowly dragging him along. She was just a little girl. All those soldiers weeping. It was a sight, she'd say."

We watch in the dark: Teddy Roosevelt dragged the length of Canoe's pool, his somber entourage passing Ricardo in his skivvies netting insects from the water's surface.

"Apparently he was an excellent horseman," Suzie adds.

Canoe reaches for another lace cookie. "Apparently," she

says. "Anyway, that was Mother's favorite story; her beginning of the end. After that, she said, it was all downhill. Bad match. Children."

"I'll tell you a bad match," Louise Cooper says.

"Oh, God, Louise," Mimi Klondike says.

"A girl from the wrong side of the tracks—"

"Here we go—" Mimi says.

"A boy from the wrong side of the tracks."

"Enter strings—" Mimi says.

"The war in Korea."

Canoe bolts unsteadily to her feet, her dress twisted around her waist and knees, togalike, so that she stumbles and falls backward, ripping a seam. We can barely see her in the dark, but we know her look: furious. She rips the seam the rest of the way, the sound remarkably loud.

"Takers?" she says.

She's a shadow but for slip and brassiere. "Last one's a rotten egg," she says, then dives, Carmen's cackle within the splash. She'll be next, of course, followed by Suzie, who says she never liked the damn thing anyway, Belgian lace or no. "I told Nursie not to bother. I planned on climbing out the first window, jumping ship. It wasn't me, I told her. I wanted a different life," she says, turning to Gay for help with the buttonhooks. "She just laughed and laughed," she says. "Why did they always laugh when you told them the truth?"

We shrug but no one can see: In this dark we're absent as the new moon, our white dresses cast onto Canoe's wrought-iron like so many five-star towels. We will all eventually follow Canoe's lead, holding our breath, jumping in—around us arms and legs, indistinguishable breasts. Couldn't we have guessed this is how it would end?

We push off the pool sides, paddle as far down as we can to the tiled bottom. We scissor our legs, gulp air, then dive below, again, before Ricardo exposes us, switching on the bright pool lights with one click.

And no doubt we are a funny sight: a school of fish too old to spawn but desperate to swim back upstream.

Hah! he says, pointing. Hah hah!

Sick Chicks

———

We arrive early at the hospice, a strange, low gray building with tinted blue windows sprawled into what was once the slope of Bishop's orchard—we can remember when we brought the children here to pick apples, the youngest insisting on riding on our shoulders, though there were bees in the lower boughs and our arms already ached from reaching.

The original intention, apparently, had been to create an office park, though the offices went mostly vacant or were occupied by suspicious businesses: acupuncturists, tanning salons, record stores. We rarely came here, and when we did we had the children, then teenagers, run in. From time to time we reminded them of when these hills were orchards, pointing out a gnarled tree, or a crumbling stone wall, though they had little interest and why should they? They were plotting their escapes, locked behind their bedroom doors, a towel wedged beneath to block the smell of marijuana, the stereo blaring.

We read in our local paper of the private venture that bought the building, the architect's rendering front-page news: HAPPY ENDING TO BLIGHTED LIFE. We knew Ginny Jones—editor, publisher, reporter—a six handicap who had come to her post under duress from a promising career in one of the smaller cities, a reporter *on camera*, she would say; we took mental note to congratulate her on the triple pun.

A hospice, it read. Swimming pool and general amenities. State-of-the-art facility.

Now here we were, the entire place too familiar. We pulled into the circular drive, the lawn jockey holding out his molding lantern, somebody's idea of welcome though it better served as a good hiding place for eggs. There were Easter egg hunts here, Christmas parties, even a Halloween dance that drew the high school students, everyone believing it a good idea to mix the near dead with the living, adolescents and children, even farm animals, of which there were several freely grazing on the front lawn. A llama named Fitzwilliam, a pig called Henrietta, Gus the sheep. We only knew this because they were Judy's chores. She woke every morning at six, her attendant wheeling her out in the early light, a bucket of grain balanced on her pencil legs. Her attendant, a large black woman known as Cookie, slept beside her in a cot, and more than once Judy had told us some of the words Cookie mumbled in her sleep. "Asparagus," Cookie would say. She slept on her back, a washcloth over her eyes, some kind of wax plug in her ears.

"Iguana," she would say.

Outside now some of the other hospice guests—they are registered as such, as if they have checked in for a long-sought-after sojourn—sit by the swimming pool, smoking; they've got no more precautions to take; they could shoot dope if they chose. There are zero rules here and truth be told, the guests look fine, happier, even, than their visitors, as they balance, fearless, on the high dive. Judy is parked near the ash can, just outside the revolving door.

"You're early," Judy says.

"We couldn't wait," Viv says.

Judy takes a last drag. "We reserved the Sunshine Room," she says, stubbing her cigarette in the sand, all of us still surprised by the look of Judy smoking. Before her diagnosis she had been our healthiest, eating six almonds each morning at breakfast, chewing Tums, cutting out articles from the *Harvard Women's Health Watch* that she posted on the board outside the Ladies' Locker. We read about estrogen replacement, mammograms, the benefits of baby aspirin. Now she smokes filterless menthols she carries in one of the cases Bambi needlepointed for all of us last Christmas, *A Woman needs a Man like a Fish needs a Bicycle* diagonally scrawled across the front. Bambi said she had read it somewhere.

Cookie appears, black and white, the tiny, ridiculous hat she's required to wear bobby-pinned to the top of her head. She bides her time and then wheels Judy through the revolving door, intended, no doubt, for CEOs or busy shoppers. Inside we follow them down the dim hallway, the light from the blue-tinted windows filigreed across the industrial carpet. We could be in a submarine, the air purged of everything but oxygen and the smell of rubbing alcohol. There may be sharks out there, and stingrays, coral reefs where brilliantly colored fish hover over their nests, their fins beating faster than their hearts; but here there is this lacy blue light and the long, uncomplicated length of the hallway to what was once the executive cafeteria, now known as the Sunshine Room. Within its solarium a fountain bubbles for contemplation. Mermaids or sea nymphs—there's been some discussion—writhe around its base in a ring-a-rosy, their hands joined, their faces turned up, expressions tortured or in ecstasy; their lips are blue. If signage is to be believed, they've been dancing since 1973.

———

The group has not entirely assembled, but they will before too long, this a highlight of the month, made better, according to Judy, by our presence. We bring a different perspective, she said. Can you imagine if it were just us sick chicks?

She has come to call herself and the other guests sick chicks; we believe it has something to do with her responsibilities with the animals and will speak to Cookie about it as soon as we get a private moment. In the meantime, the chicks file in, disoriented, the Sunshine Room brighter than anyone should have to bear. Its glass walls bead and sweat, and its piano, rolled into the corner, is grossly out of tune, the keys swollen and cracked. The sun has bleached the hummingbirds from the upholstered chairs that circle the round tables, the red from the cloth flowers in the Chinese vases at their center, the effect one of an electrified landscape. Into this they come: Mrs. William Lowell, Betsy Croninger, Cynthia Patrick, BeBe McShane, negotiating the fountain, clicking across the slippery mosaic floor in Pappagallos and patterned skirts; we have no idea what they're dying of; they look like all the women we have ever known, their faces slipping past in the silver-plated coffee urn, in the sugar bowl, the salad fork, the butter tong.

The group holds their books like so many hymnals, taking their seats with some purpose. This month's assignment: *Mrs. Dalloway.*

———

Viv taps her knife against her water glass, though no one has said a word. She's arrived with notes. "Ladies," she says, quieting us. "Ladies!" We lift our books. On the cover sits a woman sketched in a long robe and hat on a bench, steadying herself with one arm in what appears to be a garden, swirly blue flowers at her feet. The hat she wears casts a shadow over most of her face, though it is clear, from the slant of her nose, mouth, and chin, that this will not be a cheerful book. Even the colors are bland, the title a bit easy, we'd say, and not at all illuminating.

Betsy Croninger commences on a long cough and we pause, considering.

"Virginia Woolf," Viv begins, "was born in 1882 in London and died in 1941 at the age of fifty-nine." She looks at each one of us, her chin slightly tilted to match our eyes to hers above her reading glasses, as if someone might be so brazen as to challenge this fact.

"According to the internationally acclaimed novelist E. M. Forster," she continues, "Woolf, quote, 'gave acute pleasure in new ways, and pushed the light of the English language a little further against darkness,' end quote."

We recognize what Viv reads from the biographical notes on the back cover, yet still, it is good to be reminded. Viv sits back, the book spine-up on her lap, the woman on its cover now strangely sideways in her blue garden, as if she's been stuck there like a cutting, urged to root.

"Do we agree?" Viv says.

There's a long pause, in which the sound of the book club is the sound of a gurgling fountain, each mermaid or sea nymph foaming at the mouth, the water treated with a cleanser that bubbles green.

"I, frankly, was confused," Mrs. William Lowell says. "I couldn't make heads or tails."

"How so?" Viv says.

We look from one to the other as if watching a tennis match.

"I just would take issue with Mr. Forster. I wouldn't say Virginia Woolf pushed the English language anywhere. It seemed almost intentionally confusing." Mrs. Lowell shrugs and looks round to us for confirmation; we hold our faces steady, waiting to see the general direction taken by the club. We have our opinions, of course; we just prefer not to express them before a consensus has been reached.

"I like a good story," Mrs. Lowell says. "Dickens, or Austen." She sits back against the upholstered chair. She is the oldest here, her hair downy white, a sheen of it newly grown in. She wears a tiny gold pin with her initials and prefers, she said at our first meeting, the honorific. We look from Mrs. Lowell back to Viv, then back to Mrs. Lowell, who crosses her arms across her small chest, the book upside down on the table in front of her, banished to her elbow, the woman in the blue garden nowhere in sight.

"Anyone else?" Viv says too brightly.

"Fabulous," Cynthia Patrick says.

There's a sudden charge, as if somewhere someone has opened a door, flooding the room with fresh, cooler air.

"How so?" Viv says.

"All the flowers in the beginning; I liked that part."

We sit, waiting.

"And the party," Cynthia says, a slow blush spreading up her neck. "I liked the party."

"Austen knew how to tell a story," Mrs. Lowell interrupts, "and her books mean something. How many years later? You can read them again and again. In fact, I think we should read *Pride and Prejudice* next, or maybe *Jane Eyre*."

"That's Brontë," Judy says; she has made no secret of her dislike of Mrs. Lowell.

"Her, too," Mrs. Lowell says, looking around the group. "She's good, too."

"I think Cynthia was speaking," Viv says.

"Oh," Cynthia says.

"Go ahead," Viv says.

"I'm done," Cynthia says, and it's all Viv can do to bite her tongue, though in her mind she hears her mother's corrective tone: "A turkey is done." She looks at the group, then down at her notes. What has she written? What does it matter? On this page she's copied, "This moment of June." On this, "irony?" She can no longer recall what she intended to say, only the feeling of reading this book, read for the second, or possibly third time. Hadn't she suggested it after all? Hadn't she been convinced that she might bring the group around after the disaster of last month's *Ulysses*? That she might get them to see, whether they died today or tomorrow, something whole and bright about themselves? Something inexpressibly true? And now, Dickens? Charles Dickens? What could they possibly want from him?

"This moment of June," she says to fill in the silence, the incessant frothy dribbling of the fountain, the heat and smell of the Sunshine Room. She cannot bear this place, animals grazing on the lawn.

"Why 'this moment'?"

"Is there any other?" says BeBe McShane, usually so quiet. The group turns to look at her.

"I think she means there's no other than this. No future, no past. Only present."

Viv would like to kiss BeBe McShane's arthritic hands, balled like discarded tissues in her lap.

"Good," she says.

"Or at least the present of the book. That's what I found most interesting. How she plays with time, stopping time, rewinding time, parallel time—"

"'Nothing exists outside us except a state of mind,'" Viv quotes; she can't help herself.

"—right," Bebe says.

"'There was an emptiness about the heart of life; an attic room,'" Viv says.

"—uh-huh," Bebe says.

"So wouldn't it be accurate to say this is about desire?" Viv says, netting the group with her stare. "Need? *Veritas*, and by that I mean truth?" She pauses and swallows. "Rodin said," she continues, "and I quote, 'an artist worthy of the name should express *all the truth of nature*'—emphasis mine—'not only the exterior truth but also, above all, the inner truth,' end quote, so I would put forth that this is her, and by that I mean Woolf's, subject, this pursuit of inner truth, and that we, in a sense, are her vehicle, and by that I don't mean the four-wheel variety." Viv looks up from her notes and smiles; in her earlier imaginings, this is where laughter punctuates the discussion, along with nodding and intimations of agreement.

"By subject I mean we, or us. Women of a certain age," she says, her smile weakened by the general mood, which is at best confusion, overlaid by a thick quilt of boredom. "So," she says, wedging her own corrective tone higher, aiming for something light. "Did she peg us? How many of you identified with Clarissa?"

No one says a word. The other llama, the black one, Niles, wanders by, and many of the women watch his slow progress toward the farther field. Viv waits. Years ago, when she taught preschool, she had read a book about silence in the classroom, how too many teachers rush to fill in what could very well be the necessary quiet needed to generate an interesting thought. Of course her students were three-year-olds, but she had taken the advice to heart. Suffice it to say she remains hopeful, swept away, even, by Woolf's prose, as if she, too, were balanced on the eve of a party. Perhaps it is nothing more than the sight of so many women gathered, pencils sharpened.

"I've always been fond of the name Clarissa," Barbara says. "You don't hear it anymore."

The group looks from Viv to Barbara, then back to Viv again, who takes a long sip of coffee. So it's over in an instant; entirely undone. She might weep, her reading glasses heavy as a shackle around her neck. She takes another sip of coffee and wipes her mouth with the pink linen napkin provided by the hospice staff. She should have taken vows, or studied Buddhism. In a different century she would have lain in bed and died young, diagnosis *melancholia;* or written poetry and learned the piano, neutered her name.

Or perhaps she should have become a dusty scholar barricaded in the back corners of a library, sitting in a green leather chair, feet up, a stack of books to be read beside her, a notebook. She has tried, God knows, to elevate the talk, to bring it around to *ideas.* How many times had she suggested topics of conversation? How many times had she proposed they join a tour? One of her alumnae ones—excavating the ruins of Petra, sailing down the Amazon with Professor Lucinda Weissberg, studying the British dynasty on board the QE2. Now she's gone silent, mostly.

She fingers the soft edge of her edition, found last week in the attic with her schoolbooks and the notes she took in Professor Dipple's class—the Rodin line there, copied down in her own hand with the dogged precision that betrayed a student who had to work too hard, a student to whom it did not come easily, an imposter here where the other girls had attended primary schools that taught Latin, Greek, summered in Europe with great-aunts who took them to museums and on sailboats across bays. Her handwriting—so earnest, so entirely without wit or bon vivant, all her flaws implicit in its conventional slant, its loopy goodwill.

The Rodin line had been in her notes on Edna St. Vincent Millay, presumably quoted by Dipple. She pictured Dipple as she always would, tiny behind the podium, casting her voice into the well of girls as if casting a great bucket, scooping them up. Ideas! She had been Dipple's favorite, invited, even, to the home Dipple shared with the dean of students, Cilla Whitney, for Sunday supper. She had earned a solid A, and had, Dipple said, elevated the performance of the entire class. She had been a delight, *delight* Dipple's word. Viv had felt the blush begin at the back of her throat.

A fake, she had thought. An imposter.

"And there is no shame in being poor," Dipple said, knowing exactly what Viv was thinking. "No sin in that." They were eating roast chicken with sweet potatoes and string beans; they sat in the dining room of Professor Dipple's house, formal in an unrecognizable way, European, vaguely aristocratic and yet artistic as well, slightly seedy. Viv had grown used to the other formality, the formality of money, of Smith: the highly polished walnut furniture in the president's office, the floral wallpaper and the floral-covered sofas in the president's living room. There she and the rest of her class were invited to tea monthly and sat, legs crossed at the ankles, skirts tucked beneath their knees, a cloth napkin across their laps to net the crumbs. The cookies the president passed on silver platters would crumble almost as soon as you bit into them, and many of the girls figured not to bother, though she couldn't resist: the way one end had been dipped in chocolate, the other covered in pink sprinkles. She ate cookies and drank tea while the other girls talked; she watched as the president's maid refilled the tea urn, quietly scooped up the napkins that had been left on tables. When she thought of herself there, in the president's home—the other girls in their cashmere matches and suede shoes—she pictured a girl with crumbs in her lap, crumbs on her cotton blouse, her suede-patched sweater; it was as if over all of it she wore a high school letter jacket that read *Poor Girl*, as if the jacket proved the one allegiance to which she truly belonged.

Poor Girl, the jacket read in big cursive letters. She should, she supposed, have taken it off, hung it in the foyer closet along with the other girls' coats—camel hair, even mink with silky, sewn-in tags from Bonwit Teller, Lord & Taylor, Marshall Field's—but she did not, she kept it on, its color hideous, its bulk obscene, and slouched, hoping that no one would notice.

But of course Dipple did, and now here, in Dipple's strange house, the weather outside end-of-term brilliant, Viv felt again the jacket's weight, though here there were no serving maids, no flowers on the walls, no highly polished furniture. The furniture, in fact, could have used a thorough dusting, and the walls might have perked up a bit with flowers. They were a deep red, lit by two dim sconces with fringed, scorched shades that barely illumined the framed portraits of writers in the places where they lived: the famous one of T. S. Eliot at the piano, the other of Virginia Woolf in pearls, walking next to a woman introduced as Rebecca someone, in a country garden with a hound that nearly reached their shoulders.

"I myself was a refugee," Dipple said. "And poor! I didn't have two nickels to rub together, much less shoes." She speared and examined a slice of sweet potato, her stare fixed. Dipple had short gray hair and a round face unremarkable but for her eyes, which were so blue as to appear violet at times, Emma Bovary eyes, she called them, pointing out Flaubert's inconsistency. Now she chewed, the word *refugee* still ringing in that dim red room, the strangers and the dead rearranging themselves a bit on the walls, as if a strong wind had just blown through a crowd, the word so unlike the more refined Latinate words Viv had heard cast out in Dipple's lectures, the words she had so arduously copied down in her notebooks—*metaphor, illumination, consciousness. Refugee* had no place among them: too hard, too Germanic, yet Viv could not now shake the image of Dipple as a young girl, plump, since it would be impossible to imagine Dipple otherwise, on a train, her then long dark hair plaited in braids, a suitcase on her lap, kneesocks. An orphan? A Jew?

At the other end of the table Cilla Whitney smiled and salted her salad.

"Never mind all that, darling," Dipple said. "You'll make us proud."

———

"Very English," Mrs. William Lowell says.

Were they still talking about the name?

"Clarissa?" Viv says.

"The other one I like is Dahlia," Louise Cooper says. "I was desperate to name Lizzie Dahlia, and Henry said not over my dead body. He had dated a Dahlia once and apparently she was a real pain in the—"

Viv opens her book and reads the first line to come to focus. "'First the warning, musical; then the hour, irrevocable!'" she says. The group settles and looks to her: the hour irrevocable; the line, random. Yes? they seem to say, but there are no notes here, none of the wonderful Dipple bons mots— or is it bon juste?—she might pass along. Think, Viv thinks. *Think*. There are histories to every word, Dipple would say. Secret histories. You've got to unlock those doors, gaze in; you can live in those rooms if you like. But when she opens the door the room is empty, or so crammed with crap that she must shut the door quickly before an avalanche occurs.

"I think I understand that," Betsy Croninger ventures. "Within the context of the book, maybe not, but I found myself thinking of other things when I read that line. I even underlined it, see?"

They crane to view the proof; Viv can see scribbles all over the page, notes impossible to decipher from where she sits; yet still, she would like nothing more than to read them, the thought of Betsy hunched over her edition in some dim, medicinal light more than she can bear.

"Yes?" Viv says.

"It made me think of the word *cancer*. Musical at first, then irrevocable."

Betsy Croninger wears a wig of some volume, calling to mind Jackie Kennedy's Greek period. She has vividly arched eyebrows and appears to be sporting a corset beneath her blouse, a merry widow of sorts; her breasts, or what is left of them, pushed toward her throat.

"It's probably silly. It's nothing like cancer at all," Betsy says.

Viv looks down at her edition, but it is barren. And what would Dipple say to this? And what did it matter?

"I believe here she's referring to Big Ben," Viv says.

"Yes," Betsy Croninger says. "Never mind."

"The death knell?" Viv says. Was she really so bold as to say it?

"I always found that thing spooky," Judy says. "I nearly jumped out of my skin."

"Musical at first because it gave me permission somehow. To, I don't know, let go." Betsy smooths the flip of her hair, or the hair she wears. "To die, I suppose. Irrevocable in the end because I decided I didn't want to. Die, I mean. I decided I'd really rather not."

Mrs. William Lowell laughs, and then BeBe McShane and Cynthia, then Betsy Croninger herself. "I'd rather not," Betsy

Croninger repeats, laughing harder. "I've decided I'd rather not."

They laugh and so do we and then the laughing fades away.

———

We've put the book aside to talk of other things, though Mrs. Lowell prevails and the vote for next month is overwhelmingly *Pride and Prejudice*. Barbara says she will type up discussion points—she knows of a new edition with a Reader's Guide in the back! She says she looks forward to our next meeting and then we all, inexplicably, applaud.

We move on to the cookies the hospice provides, suddenly ravenous, proud of our appetites. We stretch our legs and hear our knees pop. We have aches and pains and little else, and we'll be out of here soon. To the Club for lunch, or nine holes. It's a gorgeous day and we can do as we please.

On our way out we ping the fountain, the mermaids or possibly sea nymphs still gurgling, drowning or rising impossible to tell. A few pennies rest in the scalloped bowl; they could be fished for additional wishes, but who has the inclination? One wonders who tossed them there in the first place: a child, perhaps, visiting a grandmother, the child's wish to fly, or to walk in a deep, dark wood. Or possibly a guest in the middle of the night; Judy waking Cookie, whispering, *Come on*, whispering, *Please*, Cookie reluctantly rolling her to the Sunshine Room, dark as any corner at this hour, at this moment. Judy's left hand still works—thank God for small favors, she says—and she digs in her needlepoint change purse to find the pennies there, good-luck ones she might have once wedged into loafers when she was a girl. When she was a girl?

She thinks of the moment, *this moment*, they put Melissa in her arms. She wore her red coat and a wool hat; she had stood in the parking lot for what seemed like hours, Dick pacing, before the social worker opened the door, gestured them in. She walked too quickly, forgetting patience, warmth, the baby there somewhere inside being weighed and measured, a baby now her baby. It's you, she had thought, seeing Melissa for the first time, already chubby, six months old, lying in the cradle of the scale, her fat toes in her mouth, or reaching. Why, of course; it's you, she had thought, as someone picked up Melissa and carried her across the stark room to where she stood waiting, forgetting to breathe.

She can't sleep; she can no longer sleep, and so, why not wish? She holds a penny to the thin line of moonlight, attempting to read its date, important only in the way that everything is important when dying: the penny's shine, its age, whether when she tosses it into the air it drops vertically or arcs across the fountain to ding one of the mermaids, or sea nymphs, before hitting the water; whether a splash is the sound, or whether it merely disappears: one less penny in one's change purse, hardly missed.

Her wish so transparent, so obvious after all, though she would never tempt fate as Betsy Croninger did earlier; she would never breathe a word of it.

To *live*.

Now her legs, her right arm, are stone: It determines its

own course, the doctor has said, and doggedly follows it, like a granite vein tunneling through a mountain, this eventual hardening.

———

But for now Judy merely gestures for Cookie to roll her down the long hallway toward the revolving door—she needs a cigarette; she needs a break—the others, the well ones, already skipping ahead, running down the slope that once led to the wagon trail, where in autumns past the big tractor would drag its passengers around and around the orchard, rocking under the trees weighted down with ripe apples. She would often go, sitting with Melissa or leaning against a hay bale watching her.

She cannot feel the book she has balanced on her knees, broken-spined, so that it surprises her to look down and find the woman in the blue garden staring up at her.

And you? the woman seems to say. What of you?

———

Mrs. William Lowell is dead by the next meeting. She disappeared in the middle of the night, Judy tells us; this is the way of most of them, as if the guest has had enough, will not bear another evening meal served on a plastic plate—everything expendable, To Go—and so has decided to board the night train to a better place.

Judy can't say Mrs. Lowell's death has saddened her—she

never much liked the woman—but she can say that Mrs. Lowell's death creates a hole within the group. She would have liked to have heard Mrs. Lowell's thoughts on Darcy, on Elizabeth's social predicament. She imagines Mrs. Lowell would have had a lot to say, given her own pedigree, she of the original Philadelphia Lowells. That she has ended her days in a place like this must have surprised her, though of course she never spoke of it. She had several sons, apparently, and had once been married to a man who flew his own planes and had survived Normandy; there was a First Lady in her background, and vice presidents and senators, and she had remarked—this in passing—that she had dined with Queen Elizabeth. It would have been delightful, Judy says now, to have heard what she would have had to say about Austen, whom they already knew she greatly admired.

Viv nods, as do the rest of us, suddenly picturing a spry Mrs. Lowell in pearls and mules, carrying the conversation as she no doubt once carried the conversation at dinner parties. "I like a good story," she would offer. "A beginning, a middle, and an end."

Viv suggests we take this moment before the discussion to remember Mrs. William Lowell, that we bow our heads. We dutifully agree and sit in silence, the only sound in the Sunshine Room a battering of leaves. The day's gone blustery, newly frigid. In the ghost of Bishop's orchard the trees are wrapped in burlap, their limbs bare, dead branches sawed to the joints then treated with a sticky sap to prevent infection. Goats wander among the trunks rooting for meal bugs and elsewhere, distant, a dog barks at the wind.

Warriors

This is Barbara's idea, the babies lying side by side on her new leopard-skin stole, a fur straight from Hong Kong, where apparently they don't have the reservations vis-à-vis wild animals and what does it matter, anyway, she's said, she should get some kind of compensation for Charlie's frequent traveling. They're in their birthday suits, the babies, and having none of it, their tiny tomato faces flush with rage. It is all we can do to sit on our hands; if we were breast-feeding, our breasts would leak, but we've dried them out on the advice of Dr. Spock; a little crying, he tells us, builds character.

We want character: character and brains and looks and lives led à la Amelia Earhart, who just this morning appeared in the paper, back from the disappeared, her white scarf wrapped around her thin neck, her hair bobbed. This the twenty-fifth anniversary of something. None of us has had time to read it, but the day looked important; a crowd of well-wishers stood waving. In other countries, Dr. Spock writes, mothers leave babies out in the snow and those girls grow to be warriors.

We want warriors, we'd tell him. Warriors with character. Brilliant, gorgeous warriors with character. And pilot licenses.

Anne reaches for her toes in a new trick. Advanced, Canoe warns, but she gets the genes from Buddy. Megan's fallen asleep, seeking Barbara in the smell of the leopard-skin stole, which Megan appears to be sucking. The photographer, a man whom Barbara met at the Stone Barn, a man suspiciously dandruffed and poorly suited given his reputed fame, is showing us his trick with light. He shines it over the babies' heads and they suddenly brighten, their cries calmed, fingers free from their mouths: They are four cherubs lounging on the back of a leopard, carried out of the rushes like Moses, or whomever. They have come to save us, to lead us to the promised land of Mother. Or so we're convinced; after their conceptions we've felt our world expanding, bursting out of its previous condition, what Canoe called wife-itous, newlywed-junctious, boredom-contagion. This before we knew her secret drinking, when we took her to be simply a lark. Still, there's something to it. With babies we feel oddly contained, rightfully nailed into form. No longer loose boards, a leaky vessel listing in the doldrums with a wildly spinning compass, we head straight into the wind, sails unfurled and bleached white as the diapers soaking in our bathtubs.

If nothing else they give us something to do.

———

The photographer clicks and clicks, hunched behind his funny-looking instrument, the old-fashioned kind that hooks to three spindly legs. He disappears within its cape and we murmur encouragement to our girls, the softest words we can think of, adding a *y*, or *-ie*, or *-zie*.

"Anzie," Canoe says. "Babzie. Pumpkiny. Smile!"

"Meggie," Barbara's saying. "Meggie!" She claps her hands and Megan turns her head in the opposite direction and wails.

"I think it's a tooth," Barbara says.

"Katie," Mimi Klondike says. "Ka-diddle!"

The photographer emerges from his cape, an oily strand of hair in his eyes. He may have a trace of a British accent, or it could be an affectation. "I think I've got some suitable ones," he says. "I'll be off."

He breaks down the spindly legs of the tripod, folding the big black camera into a box. We'd like him to stay for reasons we can't name. It's not often that a man we don't know strays into our midst. For now it's been nothing but women and girls, daughters all four, born within months. Down the line we will have boys, and more daughters, but the later ones, we'll agree, don't count in the same way. As Dr. Spock says, thank your lucky stars if the first is a girl. Think of her as your biblical Martha. Someone to set the house in order; to keep things straight.

———

Barbara leads the photographer to the door, where he follows the flagstone path through the Walk of Pumpkins to his Ford. The whole morning has blossomed, though the weather's autumn-gloomy. Still, the thought of ourselves as the type of women, *mothers*, who would think to hire a professional fills us with a kind of sunny pleasure. We are still young, after all; this our novelty act. We picture the results of the photographer's effort tucked in an envelope, stamped Christmas cards neatly stacked in boxes, ready to be mailed the day after Thanksgiving. We picture hearths and wreaths and our babies within boughs of evergreen: ducks in a row.

But there's so little time! Halloween's around the corner! Last year we gathered in Canoe's kitchen for popcorn balls at dusk—this before the Halloween Decency Law, the rules about store-bought, paper-wrapped candy, preferably with expiration dates—and now Barbara's weeks ahead. She's festooned her lamppost with a scarecrow, and returned to Bishop's orchard a dozen times for gourds and mums, for the pumpkins that line the flagstone. Right at this moment cider simmers on her range, cinnamon sticks like so many tiny logjams.

"Good-bye," the photographer calls, turning back to us. "God bless, then." We wave as he gets into his car and pulls away, as Barbara clips back up the walk. She shuts the door and we are once again inside together.

"What did you think?" she says, offering cigarettes from the silver bowl she keeps on her umbrella stand. We could tell you much about this house, since it's the one we tend to come to—the bag of wrapping paper and ribbon crammed in the back of the hallway closet, saved from last year out of habit, really, and Scottish blood. That the framed print of the little match girl—the poor girl standing in the newly falling

snow, her match nearly out, her fingers, one can imagine
given the shadows in the print and the bleakness of the night
beyond, frozen—is an original Currier & Ives. It hangs above
the umbrella stand, above the silver bowl of cigarettes
engraved, if one were to look carefully, with the news that
Barbara placed third in the Ladies' Nine-Hole Challenge at
the Club, 1954. We have examined it often, at dinner parties
or just in a typical afternoon, striking our own matches from
the matchbooks in the companion bowl (Honorable Men-
tion, Ladies' Nine-Hole Challenge, 1955) that read BARBARA
LYNNE & CHARLES ELLIOT, JUNE 12, 1953, MAY LOVE PRE-
VAIL WHEN ALL ELSE FAILS! We'll read it every time: the
shiny silver print embossed on the white cover. It was her
mother's idea, she's told us; she sent lines like this to the
local weekly paper and signed them Saffron. On the occasion of Barbara's wedding, she paid a local printer to print
hundreds of copies of a book she had put together, a *collection*, she called it, of life's ditties, entitled *Ditty-Not!* that she
put at every place setting. Mortifying, Barbara said, but what
could she do? Her goal remained to stay as far away from her
mother as possible, though she kept the matchbooks, she
said, because she didn't have the heart to waste them.

"He could use a dunking," Canoe says, puffing.

"Is he religious?" Judy Sawyer wants to know.

Barbara shrugs; "He's British," she says, though we know
what Judy means. There was something disconcerting about
the tone of his "God bless," a sharpened pitch to it that clouds
our earlier, sunny mood. Why would we need His blessing?
What's the photographer trying to say? It feels as if a teenager

has stolen in at midnight to roll Barbara's pumpkins down the sloped incline to her Colonial, to watch them smash, one after the other, against the grove of walnuts that blocks the light from her front bedrooms. She has thought to have the walnuts razed, but Charlie refuses, their value increasing at a faster rate than the house, an odd one for this neighborhood, a contemporary Colonial among stone Tudors. At the strangest times, she imagines how she will reclad the exterior—shake-shingle or possibly even river stone.

Gathering pumpkins, for instance, yanking them from their stalks at Bishop's as the tractor rumbles by, its passengers game but numb. This on a recent frigid morning, when she woke at dawn to Megan's screaming, to Charlie's snoring, to the no-light gloom of the walnut grove. I have to get out, she said to Charlie's back, bundling Megan in a receiving blanket and laying her across the backseat. Megan fell asleep in an instant and Barbara might have as well if not for the cigarettes: There was something soothing about driving Route 32 on a frigid morning, the sun still behind the clouds, pink, and the disk of the moon high and visible.

She blinked hard and focused on the road, on the smell and taste of the smoke. Past and before her were stone walls iced with lichen; grazing, oblivious horses; homes hidden behind juniper groves and sycamore, their stone chimneys and stone foundations and stone patios stone gray. Any moment the little matchgirl might step out from behind one of the massive oaks to offer Barbara a light; or she might see the painter, the famous one who lives nearby and is occasionally glimpsed in tall boots and a pipe, his easel under his arm, stumbling behind, sketching braids down a girl's back, knobby knees, the snow falling in the distance on a hill that looks farther, higher, better than a Currier, or an Ives.

There will be moments of panic, Dr. Spock wrote. Sheer terror, he wrote. Try to recall your prior elation as you cradled your Martha to sleep; if that doesn't work, lock yourself in the bathroom and cry.

"Knock, knock," someone says. We're in the kitchen drinking the mulled cider, the girls lying on the leopard-skin stole in the center of the linoleum, their fingers in their mouths. They are not yet at the age to crawl, and so we have surrounded them with pots and pans, thick wooden sticks, a ticking egg timer. Always stimulate, Dr. Spock suggests, a simple kitchen tool is best. But they seem more interested in Barbara's kitchen wallpaper, a pattern of sunflowers and windmills at which they blindly stare. Are they blind? we've been discussing, or do they already know our faces? Could they, say, pick us out in a crowd as Mother? There's something about our smells, Dr. Spock says, though God knows we've lately gone identical, Chanel No. 5 on cuff and collar.

"Yes?" Barbara says.

"It's Louise!" Louise Cooper calls from somewhere; she is not of our set but she aims to be. No doubt she's carrying an offering.

"Louise!" Barbara says, standing and stubbing out her cigarette. She clicks into the hallway and returns with poor

Louise, out to here and wearing the mask of pregnancy. This is an unfortunate affliction, says Dr. Spock, not particularly rare and harmless, of course, but nonetheless embarrassing to the carrier—skin pigmentation darkening to nearly black around the eyes and over the bridge of the nose. Poor Louise looks like a bloated, feral animal tottering in behind Barbara, her offering, we can see now, wrapped in tinfoil.

"Louise!" we say.

"Look at them!" she says, noticing our daughters. "How adorable!"

"We had a photo shoot!" Barbara says, setting the wrapped plate before us and gloriously unrolling the foil. We stub out our cigarettes and reach.

"How wonderful!" Louise says. She lumbers down and smiles and we smile back, our smiles strained by our full mouths. It is difficult to look directly at her, the skin not only darkened but spotted, blotched: Louise generally so glamorous. It is she who once attracted the most attention from our husbands, her ancestry Irish, or something exceedingly healthy, her backhand unbeatable.

"The news is I'm dilated," she says. "Dr. Wells thinks it will be any minute."

"Dr. Wells doesn't know his ass from his elbow. He could practically stick his fist in and Anne didn't budge for weeks," Canoe says. "These are delicious!"

"I don't remember a thing," Mimi Klondike says. "How can you remember any of it?"

"Nature wants us to forget," Judy Sawyer, childless, adds.

"Who?" Barbara says.

"Nature," Judy says.

"Nature?" Barbara says. "I remember *everything*. Charlie said he could hear me clear down the hall. He went to the parking lot; couldn't stand my screaming. The things I said! They give you the truth serum. I told Dr. Wells he looked like Mickey Mouse and that the nurse looked like Dopey."

"Oh, baby," Canoe says, turning back to Louise. "It'll be a breeze!"

"And me like this," Louise Cooper says. We eat the cookies; they're tinged with something, whiskey? and shrug.

"You can hardly notice," Mimi says, chewing.

"Henry's mother says it has to do with breeding," Louise Cooper says. "Something to do with the Irish."

"Breathing?" Judy wants to know.

"She said she'd never known of anyone so stricken," Louise says.

"Tell her to take a long walk down a short pier," Canoe says.

Louise smiles and rubs her eyes with the back of her hand and we are hopeful, for a moment, that she might streak it away, that possibly, when her hand returns to her lap, the mask of pregnancy will have magically vanished, but it is there, like a tattoo, and strangely, we can no longer imagine Louise without it.

———

The surprise is it's pumpkin soup. Pumpkin! A recipe Barbara found in last Sunday's Home section devoted to fall flavors. Add the seeds! it advised. Seeds to salads, seeds to soup, seeds to your roasted, flavorful meats. Seeds suggest the harvest, in turn suggesting spring, birth. We stare at our girls lying on the kitchen floor and crunch, smiling, the girls' beauty remarkable. Perhaps this is why we are less than surprised when the photographer reappears. He's had trouble leaving, no doubt, leaving us, leaving the babies, leaving this scene of bounty.

But no, he says. He's forgotten something. He stands in the middle of Barbara's kitchen, smelling vaguely foreign. He has shed the tripod and the clunky black box, and we see now that he wears a dandruffed velvet vest, and that a chain disappears into his breast pocket to a weighted thing, a vial of opium, perhaps—he's an artist!—or a pocketwatch etched with the initials of his great-grandfather.

"Can we help you find it?" Barbara says, though he seems to have no idea what. He's spellbound within the sunflowers and windmills—there must be hundreds—smitten by Louise Cooper.

"Can we help you find it?" Barbara repeats.

"What?" he says, breaking away.

"The thing."

"Oh," he says. "There," he says, pointing to what any of us might have taken for a can opener on Barbara's counter. "My light meter." He makes no motion to move and then Louise looks up, perhaps sensing his attention.

"Is it real, then?" he asks.

"What?" she says.

"That," he says, fingering his nose.

"Oh," she says, her hand fluttering up to her mask, gingerly touching the skin as if she worries it might stain her fingertips. "Yes. Unfortunately, yes."

"I've never seen one," he says.

"They're rare," she says, "but not that. One in several hundred."

Her hand returns to her lap, or what would be her lap if it weren't for the child; we know now a little: how the baby has positioned itself in its preparation to be born, how its tiny arms, its hands, first appeared as buds, how its lungs, its heart, its spine were initially outside its skin and then, like a backward blossoming, folded inward. So much can happen! The delicacy of life! We've read the books, looked for hours at the pictures. It is never not fascinating. Even now we could lay our heads on Louise Cooper's stomach and feel that baby's heartbeat, watch its tiny elbow, or possibly knee, glide across her skin. The glory of that! It was good to be reminded. A tabula rasa, Esther Curran called it, though she wouldn't want one in a million years. They're your blank canvases. Our tiny captains, we could tell her, steering us farther away.

"Would you mind?" the photographer is saying, but we've missed what.

"I suppose not," Louise says. "If the other girls don't care."

"Care?" Judy Sawyer wants to know.

"He wants to take my picture," she says.

"Who?" Barbara says, but the photographer has already slipped out, scurrying down the Walk of Pumpkins to his Ford, where his equipment, no doubt, sits at the ready.

The photographer pulls one of Barbara's barstools into the center of her kitchen; the babies at last sound asleep, or quieter, nestled within the cushions of the den sofa. We can hear them easily from where we stand watching. The photographer asks Louise to perch on the stool, which she does awkwardly, one foot on one of the spindles; now he holds the light meter this way and that, turning the stool and repositioning Louise. Louise is being a good sport; she's Irish, after all. She's removed her shoes and her earrings at his request, changed into one of Barbara's old robes. He's asked her to undo her hair from its chignon: a glorious bottle-red.

"Tilt down—" the photographer is saying.

"This?" Louise says, looking up.

"Down, chin down," he says. "I want to see your eyes."

Louise's eyes, we'd agree, are her best feature. Normally, she accentuates them with a pale green shadow, though now it looks as if she's rubbed them with tar. Louise looks out as if an animal trapped in a deep hole.

"Beautiful," the photographer says.

"Don't smile," he says.

It's been nearly an hour. The girls are crying in the other room but we have fed them and changed them and Dr. Spock strongly recommends that if all the basic, necessary elements have been covered, one resist the natural urge to coddle.

Louise sits with her knees up, her hands clasped around her legs: She's tilted her head this way and that, smiled or not. At one point he wanted her hair over her face. Barbara's suggested our new favorite, bourbon punch, and a pitcher's been made and emptied; in the living room, a foursome play bridge. We might still be at school, in our social rooms, or we might be at the Club in the old crones' lounge. It's gotten more gloomy or perhaps the day has simply passed in the way days pass now—all of us together, not for companionship, exactly, or high regard, but because we're in the same boat.

Out Barbara's windows the remaining sycamore leaves brighten, possibly glow, against the half-dark and occasionally a walnut thunks the roof, breaking the photographer's concentration. He's trying to concentrate, he's told us; he's trying to find the form.

"I'd say it was staring you smack in the face," Canoe says.

The photographer turns to Canoe. He might have brilliant eyes, though who could tell behind those glasses? Buddy Holly thick, myopic. His hands hold the camera strap around his neck and they are too white, we can see from here, hairless and soft.

"Could you do something about that crying?" he says.

"What crying?" Canoe says. She has mastered Spock. She's his greatest disciple. Ask her anything and she can tell you exactly where—in the world according to Spock—you might find the answer.

The photographer blinks and turns back to Louise, his shoulders hunched.

"How old are you?" he asks her.

"Twenty-three," she says. "Just turned."

"Is this your first child?" he says. He is taking pictures as he questions her, and from somewhere he has found a smaller camera, so that he moves as he speaks.

"Of course," Louise says, laughing.

"Still, Mrs. Cooper," he says, and she straightens, oddly unaccustomed to the name though she has heard it so often. Each time it recalls the look of Henry's mother, a scratchy square of wool known as Mother Cooper.

"Is your husband pleased?"

"My husband?" Louise says.

"I assume there's a husband," he says.

"Henry," she says.

"Is Henry pleased?" he asks, again.

Louise holds an expression as if he has asked her to, though it's an awkward one, and we can't imagine it will lead to good pictures.

"I never inquired," she says. "I assume so. Yes."

"Were you born here?"

"Oh, God, no. I'm from Detroit."

"Your father in the auto industry?"

"Both parents."

"A working mother, then."

"Every day of her life."

"Tough for a child."

"I did okay."

"Siblings?"

"Two brothers."

"Autoworkers?"

"One. The other killed in France."

The photographer stands—he's been on one knee—and takes off his glasses. He rubs them with what looks like a handkerchief and returns it to his trouser pocket. We watch, forgotten; we never knew a thing about Louise Cooper's past, or, for that matter, about any of our pasts. We tend to look ahead, to speak of present things: our husbands' jobs, the sleep cycles of our babies.

The photographer squats.

"Were you close?" he says.

"Who?"

"You and your brother," he says.

"Oh, God, who knows. He was my big brother," Louise says.

She pulls a corner of the robe over her knee; whatever the fabric, there's a sheen and it tends to slip off her legs.

"Devon," she says.

"Hmm?"

"That was the town. Somewhere in the south of France. I've always wanted to go there," she says. "But Henry doesn't like French food."

"Your parents?" he says.

"Yes?"

"They pleased about all this?"

"All what?"

"Your life with, Harry?"

"Henry."

"The baby," he says.

"I imagine so."

"Imagine?"

"I don't hear from them."

"No, you wouldn't."

"I'm sorry?" Louise Cooper says.

"Nothing," the photographer says. "I'm getting the picture."

She looks at him. "May I have a cigarette?"

"Done," he says, standing. He reaches inside the pocket of his vest and draws from it a single cigarette, which he lights and hands to Louise.

"My father put me on the train to Chicago, actually," she says, smoking. "I was seventeen years old. I don't believe he had any idea where I was going, but I said I had a ticket and had to get to the station and he drove like a bat out of hell." She laughs and the smoke curls up around her face. "He said, 'Good luck, baby,' and held the door open for me, the little door to my compartment. He said, 'Knock 'em dead.'"

"Knock who dead?" the photographer says. He sits cross-legged on the linoleum, cradling the camera.

"I have no idea," Louise Cooper says.

———

There is a witching hour, as any mother knows. The girls have been given their bottles but they are out of sorts: We hold them and jiggle, pat their backs. On any other day this would be the time to leave, to return to our own houses, not so far from here, at the end of similar drives, within trees, atop mowed lawns. We would bathe our girls then, as Dr. Spock suggests—routine is what Marthas crave—and wait for six o'clock, when our husbands, collectively, return from the trenches. We call it the trenches as we hand them their drinks. This is our joke, and theirs, and it never fails to make us laugh.

How were the trenches? we say, though we know better: We know they sit at wide desks far from here or wait in lines at restaurants for lunch—a grilled steak and a martini, or a gin and tonic. They come home generally pleased, a day's work behind them, an evening at home before them. In such a mood they cradle the baby as we finish cooking and set the table.

But today we do not leave: Today we spend at Barbara's, oblivious of time. We stand with our girls out of the photographer's path, apart from Louise. We have made ourselves invisible at the photographer's request, our sound the sound of the babies' crying.

Louise sits in Barbara's zip-up robe, a pair of Barbara's slippers on her feet. She has moved to a more comfortable chair, though she is still in the kitchen, the empty plate of what she brought beside her scattered with crumbs and cigarette butts. A familiar rooster clicks on the wall, its electric minute hand slowly turning; every hour it cock-a-doodle-doos. The photographer waits it out and then continues talking.

"And this is when you left Danny," he says.

"Henry presented a better opportunity," Louise says. "I was tired of being a Democrat." She has been talking of someone else, someone from her Former Life in Detroit, a boy we picture as taller than Henry, handsome in a better way. In our minds' eye he wears a jaunty hat and workman clothes, and his hands, though raw red from the cold of those winters, are beautiful. We picture Louise and Danny in a warehouse somewhere, behind a plowed field studded with the rusting carcasses of automobiles—barely visible, like half-buried treasure. They are inside or outside, it doesn't matter, and they are necking like crazy, Danny's beautiful hands on Louise's shoulders, Louise's eyes closed or maybe open, surprised by what she has agreed to or reluctantly refused. It could go either way: We are well aware of Louise's reputation.

————

"A shame," the photographer says; he is reloading.

"In certain circles," Louise says.

"Have you been in touch?"

"Hmm?" Louise picks at the crumbs with a wet finger.

"With Danny?"

"Oh, God, no. Danny?" she says. "He disappeared years ago. Died in Korea, apparently. Are we still talking about Danny?"

It's gone dark in Barbara's kitchen and the photographer has set up equipment, lights clipped to the pot rack. In the glare Louise's eyes look as if they've been painted white. She stares wide-eyed at the bottom of her hole. Who can say when this animal will be caught? If there's anything to be done to coax it forward? From time to time it slowly blinks. Disbelieving, perhaps, its impending entrapment. "Move to the left, darling," the photographer says. "And unzip, then."

"Hmm?" Louise says, turning from the remnants on the plate, a stray.

"The robe, baby. Just a tad."

Louise looks at us but she might be onstage; the lights blinding. Can she see us from there? Does she recognize us as her friends, her compatriots, on the other side?

The photographer moves toward her but Louise has already reached for the zipper, the robe partially off her shoulders. Her breasts are huge, their nipples black as her mask. This is the first thing. Then, a line of hair that begins at her navel. Did we all darken this way? Discolor and expand before we split in two? It's difficult to remember who we were before; mothers are willing amnesiacs, Dr. Spock says. It's nature's way. Still, we hold our restless babies and stare, seeing something once lost, something vaguely familiar.

The photographer murmurs encouragement. "Louisie," he's saying. "Sugar, Louis-ie," he says, moving around her. "Yes, sweetie," he says, "that's right," as Louise, silent and elsewhere—in Danny's arms? Racing with her father to the train, afraid of missing, what? Her destiny?—tilts her head back so far you can no longer see the black mask of pregnancy, simply the brilliant white of her throat, the flash the photographer now uses to erase her again and again. Each time our eyes must readjust. And where are we now? And who is this before us? Oh yes, Louise Cooper, poised on the cusp of what Spock calls our glorious journey, our sweet and rightful path.

Then the robe, slipped or nudged, falls entirely off Louise's shoulders, and she is eclipsed by her enormous belly, one we cannot take our eyes off until we too see what she must feel—the water trickling down Louise's legs, puddling on Barbara's linoleum. Louise gasps and jolts up, her hands clutching the hurting place, her eyes huge within their mask, terrified.

Back When
They Were Children

———

"Inspiration arrived in the shower," Canoe announces. "In a nutshell: hats. Girls in hats with floppy brims." She had thought of it as a row, she says, linear, like the Rockettes, only not so leggy. "What I mean is a parade," she says. "A contest, of sorts."

We look from Canoe to the girls, who stand before the long table shifting their colt legs. Then we turn back to Canoe. The hats, eight total, are stacked on her head, one fitted inside the other. They are plain straw hats, the kind discovered in the sale bin. She purchased them at Fleishmann's, she has told us; a store we know well and one that has, for the past few months, a LOST OUR LEASE sign curled in its window among dusty chocolate bunnies and sugar chicks. This is where we bought supplies for our own projects last fall: yarn in bright colors, a quilting ring, a glue gun. We were on the cusp of a new phase, Canoe said, a shifting of the paradigm. It often happened in one's thirties, early forties, she told us. Creativity arriving in a burst of flames. She knew too many stories to count. The future looked bright!

Anyway, Fleishmann's was offering craft classes and if we'd follow, Canoe said, she'd lead. We would be studying under the direction of Jean Weiss, the owner of the Brush & Palette, who apparently taught the classes in exchange for a daily BLT and fries.

Those fall days, those *lost halcyon* days, Canoe remembers, we sat at a conference table near the lunch counter: the smell hamburgers and fried onions, the sound spoons on coffee cups. The counter was crowded with customers we would have recognized if we had bothered, but we did not. We were good students. The best one could hope for, Jean Weiss said afterward. Those days, those *lost halcyon* days, the sun came through the store's front plate-glass window in a particular way, and our Main Street felt lively, the ting of the little bell that hung from the swinging front doors suggesting commerce and trade, a certain lived life. Canoe's idea had caught on and there was not one among us who did not picture her creations arresting Jean's eye; she would offer us a special solo show at the Brush & Palette, where we had frequently attended Esther's exhibits, first a collection of still lifes, distorted and vague, as if we were viewing them through a stranger's glasses, and then a selection from the Middle Period, as she called it, of the monochromes—orange, blue, red—experimentations in Nothingness, she said. (Esther's mother-in-law, Sydney, had recently returned from an island in the Philippines and had apparently spoken to her of the teachings of Buddha.) Esther's final show, arranged posthumously by Jean from what remained in Esther's studio, was clearly influenced by the New York Abstract Expressionists and the Chicago School, or so Jean wrote in "Notes from Jean," the program she left on the plant stand near the front door. Regardless, we couldn't make heads or tails: It looked as if Esther had taken all the trash that had collected in the ruts of her long drive, blown there in the winters after Walter's death, and simply glued it to unframed canvases. There were hundreds of them, or so it felt, gigantic and miniature: They covered the walls, rolled onto the floor—everywhere you looked, debris. A few were sprayed with paint, varying hues of brown and black and white, and to those we found ourselves gathered. "'She lost her taste for color in later years,'" Gay Burt read from "Notes from Jean," and for an instant we pictured a young Esther, her hands and mouth smeared with yellows and blues, gorging.

———

Canoe clears her throat. The point is expression, she's saying. One must express what one feels on the *inside*.

We look at our girls, standing as if at attention, though Canoe's own daughter, Anne, looks down as if spying a penny in the dirt, flushed with embarrassment at her mother before her friends—eight hats on her head—or the excitement of her birthday party. Who can tell? Anne stares at her shoes: hideous plastic straps on cork platforms. Our girls wear the same, and rabbit fur coats lined in garish silk, bought at the mall, where on Saturdays they meet and walk for hours, ghosts within the artificial light. What they feel inside? Who could possibly know?

But here we're in sunshine! And scrubbed breeze; the day nothing short of glorious. Most of the crocuses have come and gone, but the lilac are newly clipped and in bloom, each purple, seed-sized petal obscenely fragrant. (We gathered the branches at Canoe's request, dropping stem after stem into Anne's horse buckets. And forsythia, too, and the daffodils that sprout willy-nilly between the flagstone steps to Canoe's pool, Mimi Klondike mistakenly decimating a stand of iris.) Everything seems possible, even our girls in hats of their own making, careening down Canoe's drive in Canoe's Woody to town, Main Street, she's explained, the Brush & Palette, to be exact, where we'll demand of Jean Weiss who is the fairest of them all, because none of us could possibly choose, given that we are mothers, and they our daughters.

───────

"You want us to wear a hat?" Lizzie Cooper says.

"Yes," Canoe says. "Of your own making," she says. "Any way you wish. I've bought embellishments. It'll be fun!" She points toward the bowls of sequins, feathers and cloth flowers laid out; there are also stacks of women's magazines, felt-tipped markers, scissors, glue.

Lizzie shrugs and sits down at one of the folding chairs arranged around the table. The other girls shuffle in beside her, Megan laughing. "What?" Katie Klondike wants to know. "Later," Megan says.

———

In a matter of years they will be gone, but now they are twelve, or just about. Their legs have sprouted and their arms are hairy and Megan, Barbara's first, has already started to bleed.

In truth they terrify us.

This they know, though they bide their time. With sweetness they obtain material goods: saddleshoes and cheerleading skirts, private lines on which they dial boys we've never met. How the time has flown, et cetera, et cetera, and no, we wouldn't wish it back; or most of it. The snow days, perhaps. The girls on sleds with mittened fingers. Rosy cheeks. In the distance there'd be sleigh bells, evergreens strung with lights as the girls tumble down Toboggan Hill, our dogs bounding barking after them. In the twilight a winter silence descends, the girls brushing themselves off as a weighted bow drops its armload of snow, cardinals at the feeder.

Or perhaps this is just how we remember it; the girls say they were freezing and we too quickly disappeared, smoking cigarettes in the kitchen.

———

We retire poolside to let the girls work. Canoe suggests wine, since she has a quiche in the oven, and the day, though sunny, takes random turns to brisk. "How those girls can stand open-toed shoes is beyond me," Canoe says.

"Anyway," she says, "what I feel inside is parched. I need reserves. And a light."

We join her, waving the smoke away from our faces. Up the hill we hear laughing and picture the girls cutting and pasting, though they are more likely talking about us, sneaking their own cigarettes. They squint into the smoke, their eyeshadow, bought at the mall's Dollar Store, pink; white in the crease of the lid, brown, with glitter, just below the arch of their finely plucked eyebrows. Hideous, true, but who can stop them? It's as if they are powered by an invisible force, some kind of centrifugal magnet—a thick, molten ball within the earth's hard surface. They would rather shop indoors, eat caramel corn from greasy paper bags, sip an Orange Julius. Feel inside? We haven't the slightest idea, haven't known for years, in fact, not since scraped knees and splinters. Or the time the others ganged up and they wept in our laps. We can recall that like yesterday: the knot of pain we felt at their exclusion. What we wouldn't do to soothe them, stroking the damp curls away from their foreheads and hot cheeks, kissing their small, knuckled fingers; they were the only things we loved, these soft creatures, so easily bruised. We called them by their pet names, served them ice cream in circus dishes.

But this was back when they were children; now they're something else.

"I told her in her teen years she can do what she pleases," Canoe is saying. Apparently Anne had begged for a party at the roller rink, the kind Katie Klondike had last month, where we dropped the girls off at the front doors, then picked them up a few hours later, their clothes smelling of stale smoke—ours or theirs?—their eyes too bright.

"When I was her age I would have given my right arm for this party. The shower inspiration story was bullshit. I was trying to rally the troops."

She takes a long drag on her cigarette and squints. She is fair, Canoe, her skin so freckled as to appear molted. She has always been the athlete among us—she can whack the ball two hundred yards.

"I had this idea for my twelfth birthday that I wanted all my friends to make hats and that we would go on a hat parade and that some stranger would choose whose hat was the best, and of course it would be mine, given how the day was mine and, at the time, the world."

"On a plate," she says, smiling. "Wedgwood china."

"So?" Mimi Klondike asks.

"Hmm?" Canoe says.

"Did you win?"

"Oh, God, win? My mother had already booked the club. It was a tea. White gloves, white anklet socks. The boys hid in the bathroom so we danced with each other. I got stuck with Missy Wentworth, six foot eight and all feet, she didn't know to lead or follow. My toes were black and blue for weeks.

"I never forgave Mother. Sat in my room and blinked for hours. It was a habit I had. Drove her out of her gourd."

"MO—THER!" It's Anne's voice from up the hill.

"I'm summoned," Canoe says, stubbing her cigarette beneath her flat. We watch her jog up the flagstone steps, the ric-a-rac around the hem of her wraparound skirt uneven, we note, remembering our own failed attempts, though to her credit Jean Weiss had been encouraging.

"Ladies," she said. This Jean, the first day, after we'd gone around the table to introduce ourselves, though we'd known one another and Jean for years, Jean through Esther, one of Esther and Walter's parties. Jean had arrived with her mother, a small woman named Bettina who spoke with a Polish accent and oddly drank too much, though we'd always heard that Jews don't drink. She had her reasons, apparently: everything a great mystery. We were never told why they moved here in the first place, though we understood that they knew something about Art and planned to renovate the old Beardsley shoe store to a gallery.

"Did they know that Wyeth lived just down the road?" we asked them.

"Yes," they said. "It had been mentioned."

"Did they plan on showing his work?"

"They hadn't yet decided," they said. "He might be too representational for their tastes."

Representational. The word hung around Esther and Walter's party, exotic as hashish. It made us feel sophisticated and boorish at the same time.

———

Now Jean's mother was dead some five years, and Jean ran the Brush & Palette on her own. We didn't understand most of the work she exhibited, but we were invited to the openings and would go, from time to time, to see what was new, attempting to decipher the "Notes from Jean."

Yet here we were in the range of her eagle eye, our hands poised over the ric-a-rac, our needles threaded. We would start at the very beginning, Jean said.

"A very good place to start," Canoe said.

We laughed and Jean looked up.

"The Sound of Music," Bambi said.

"'Doe-a-deer, a female deer,'" Viv sang.

Jean looked back to her lap, where the square of material she had chosen from the heap held three widths of ric-a-rac and examples of various stitches with which to pin them down. "I never much cared for that film," she said.

And it was only later, of course, that we remembered Liesl's infatuation with the Nazi.

———

Ric-a-rac, macramé, the Golden Age, Canoe would recall, of ceramics. Those were the later October weeks, when inspiration rained down on us as lightly as the leaves from the maples on Main Street—this before the winter blight and the Arboreal Vermin Laws. We retrieved the girls from sports with dried clay on our hands, sketched ideas on cocktail napkins, woke with a start, our hearts beating. Jean convinced Mimi Klondike and Barbara to embark on the Nine

Muses, the Muses' robes draped in cracked folds. Still, a few survived the kiln unscathed, emerging from the ashes whole if not beautiful. We fired up a storm, let our hands speak for our minds. This Jean's expression.

Let your hands speak, Jean would say. Turn your hearts to your hands, what you feel inside.

And now, up the hill, we hear Canoe repeating Jean's words, the wind carrying her voice down to where we sit.

"Ladies," she yells suddenly. "Come see these creations!"

We tromp up to where the girls are gathered, the hats before them like so many tiny mountains. The girls work steadily, seeming mildly occupied, or rather, resigned to finish; we have dropped all hope for *enthusiasm*, per se; some years ago they let us know they were too old for that. This is the best they can do: a shrug of the shoulders, a nod of the head. We watch as they cut and paste, glue sequins to the floppy brims. We too would rather be elsewhere, a glass of wine in our hands.

Barbara squats next to the place where Megan sits, shoulders hunched.

"Excellent," Barbara says of Megan's work, then she squints up at us.

"Megan just needs encouragement," she says, though she has told us all this before: encouragement, she says. And willpower. If Megan would wash her hair more thoroughly, lose her baby fat. For Megan's birthday, Barbara balanced a half head of lettuce in a confectioner's box, pink candles stuck in its leafy folds.

"Look at these pictures!" Barbara's saying. "Look at what she's found in the magazines!"

Megan pushes her bangs off her forehead and stares up at us, then over at her mother, whom she resembles, beneath her bulk, in an uncanny way. She has crudely cut photographs from the pages of the magazines and glued them onto the straw, the pictures bumpy, overglued, each one of a girl modeling a swimsuit.

"Aren't you proud of yourself?" Barbara says, and we recognize it as pure Spock: Don't be proud of them, he says, tell them to be proud of *themselves*. Megan ignores Barbara and returns to her crucified *Glamour*.

"Look, Mommy," Linda says.

Suzie applauds. "Reminds me of something the Queen Mum would wear."

"I made it," Linda says, stabbing at her glasses, cat's eyes, with the back of one hand.

"I'm well aware," Suzie says.

Linda looks at Suzie, her eyes huge behind the thickness of the glass.

"They're all beautiful," Canoe says too loudly. "Bravo!"

"Bravo!" Mimi Klondike says.

"Please," Katie Klondike says.

"Please, what?"

"I mean, look at mine," Katie says.

"It's a work of art," Mimi says.

"It's a piece of shit," Katie says.

The other girls stop their gluing as if violently slapped; Katie, apparently, still having difficulty with the divorce.

"Well, it's certainly original."

We look at Katie's creation: She's attempted to glue on the cloth flowers, though the material has bunched into an indecipherable glob.

"An original piece of shit," Katie says.

"Young lady—" Mimi says.

"Can I have another hat?" Katie asks Canoe.

"Only one per customer," Canoe says, brightly.

"This is bullshit," Katie says.

"Katherine Suzanne Klondike," Mimi says.

"What?" Katie says.

"March," Mimi says.

Katie takes her time pushing back from the long table. "Sorry, Anne," she says. "Later, Lizzie," she says, the two, we know, the best of friends. A few years from now, they'll be caught buck naked in the Colin family cemetery, their boyfriends—brothers who have dropped out of high school and spent time in a juvenile center for selling marijuana—hiding within the shattered glass of the Colin mausoleum. The guard who catches them will write a report that will appear in the local newspaper, including the words statutory rape.

———

Mimi and Katie's departure puts a temporary pall across the day, though the clouds soon blow through and by early afternoon the sun feels close to a summer sun. The girls have spread tinfoil over the hard folds of some album covers from Canoe's collection—the Dave Clark Five, we recognize—and sit angled, their long legs propped on the table, the shiny covers just beneath their chins to catch the rays and tan their faces. We have killed the wine, ravaged the quiche. The girls picked at the sandwiches Canoe served, fanned out on a tray. They're on diets, they explained, something about hard-boiled eggs and bananas, but when Canoe reappears with the cake they lunge for it, scooping tipfulls of icing, the pink and purple flowers that bloom along its brim. A hat cake, of course, Canoe a sucker, she says, for a theme.

She claps her hands to get our attention. We have all been flagging and would in truth like to crawl back to our beds.

"It's time!" Canoe says. "Ladies!" Canoe says, clapping again. "Let's parade!"

The girls look up from where they've been drifting, their faces already red, scorched from the unfamiliar sun, greasy with a concoction of baby oil and iodine.

"What?" Lizzie Cooper wants to know.

"I have arranged for a judge," Canoe says. "A professional. Let's not keep her waiting. Come on!" Canoe says.

We urge the girls to follow, because how can we not? She our hostess, our friend. She leads them to the drive and gestures for them to pile into her Woody, the all of them squeezing into the backseat and rearback, their hats on their heads, their bony knees raised or folded to fit like so many origami cranes.

"Peace," Barbara calls as they pull out; she holds up the

two-finger sign, her gaze fixed on Megan, slumped in the front seat for obvious reasons, vis-à-vis her width.

"Meggie's coming into her own," Barbara says, turning back to us. "She'll be fine."

———

We park near the Brush & Palette, parallel on Main Street. This is not our town's finest hour. Most of the stores have been pilloried by the mall, and once Fleishmann's closes, there will be little left. The girls wouldn't be caught dead wandering these sidewalks with their mothers: et cetera, et cetera. Still, we take Canoe's lead—she's always been our most vigorous, even sauced—and march up the sidewalk, our town balanced on the crest of a hill. Where the maples once grew are now light poles festooned with streamers. A banner that reads MAY MAYHEM!: SOLDIER'S FIELD, MAY 7, 5 P.M.–9 P.M. flaps across the intersection of State.

It seems like years since we've been out in this harsh daylight, and we feel a little queasy thinking of what Canoe has up her sleeve. She emerges from the Brush & Palette, steering the girls across the street toward Fleishmann's— apparently Jean is on her lunch break. She holds the front door wide open as they shuffle in, and by the time we catch up we can see them making their way through the bolts of bold-colored fabric and the plastic floral arrangements toward the grill. There are few customers and those we see we don't recognize, except Jean, sitting hunched at the counter. We'd know Jean anywhere, even from behind, and for a moment we feel the anticipation we felt in those *lost halcyon* days of autumn, presenting our handiwork with a mix of embarrassment and pride, wondering if perhaps there was some talent here, something that had, heretofore, been overlooked.

But she never mentioned it.

"Jean!" Canoe calls. Jean rolls around on her stool. She is a small woman, her hair cropped short and bleached white. She dresses in dark wool pantsuits, even on a day as warm as this one, and wears her signature pin on her lapel: a gold artist's palette, its paint a series of rhinestones. We've heard rumors that in Paris, Jean spied for the Allies, was Hemingway's lover, that she had once, like so many of us, been a beauty, but it is hard to believe anything of Jean except what is Here Right Now: Fleishmann's grill, the smell of old grease lilting about, drifting on the dust motes, settled on the ball of sweaters and scarves shoved into the cardboard box marked BARGAIN BASEMENT at the end of the counter.

There is nothing we don't know of this store; nothing we couldn't find with our eyes closed. The goldfish are in the basement with the parakeets and hamsters, lining the corner marked PET SHOPPE; we have come for them so many times we can't count, our girls with tearstained faces, flushed cheeks, promising, swearing they will try harder this time, they will not forget to clean the algae from the tanks, to change the filter, to measure the fish food more carefully: *yes*, they say, *please*, they say, and we are suckers for their small smiles. We would take them anywhere, buy them anything they asked for, not to hear their sobs. Yes, we say, it's time, then fine, we say, the training bras are behind the Evening Wear in the Lingerie Department, we say, leading them to the heap of cotton undershirts and underpants on the display table within the hanging rows of flesh-colored cups, inches thick. Yes, we say, all right then, here, we say, standing in front of the Beauty Salon near Hardware and Grills, the saleswoman waiting with a poised lipstick, the button on her smock reading ASK ME ABOUT YOUR MAKE-OVER. And where had we seen her before? Checking bags at the Safeway? No matter: Our girls do their part, turning their gorgeous faces away from us, pouting their lips.

And Here Right Now, our girls lining up for the contest, entirely indifferent to the judge. They are as near to gone as Fleishmann's, FOR RENT all over their faces. They'd take any life over this one; they can't wait to be had.

———

"Well, well," Jean says, getting shakily to her feet. There are the remains of a BLT on her plate, some cold coffee at the bottom of her cup.

"Aren't they fabulous!?" Canoe says. "They did it themselves!"

"I should say," Jean says.

"I bought the embellishments, the rest was entirely their idea."

The girls smirk. Lizzie coughs.

"Who's the birthday girl?" Jean asks.

"Right here!" Canoe says. "Anne!"

Anne straightens her shoulders as if called to attention; her hat is set at a rakish angle, no doubt to hide the bloom of acne on her cheeks and forehead, or perhaps to better display the horses she has drawn galloping around the brim. Anne has always been a homely girl, horsey even before she knew how to ride. The acne has not helped matters, and she's developed a habit of biting her bottom lip.

"You?" Jean says, peering at Anne beneath her hat.

"Yes, ma'am," Anne says; the line of girls snicker, Megan's more a snort. She has taken the opportunity to rest on one of the counter stools, the ridiculous hat jammed on her head.

"So, you like horses?" Jean says.

"Yes, ma'am," Anne says.

"My, my. Well, that's certainly a beauty," she says. "And my mother used to say it took no money to have manners." Jean glances over at the rest of our girls, who have joined Megan at the counter; they twirl the stools, their minds elsewhere. What they think inside? We haven't a clue, and, quite frankly, would rather not know.

"Congratulations," Jean says, shaking Anne's limp hand. "It's obvious who deserves first place."

"Hear, hear!" Canoe says, clapping. She is lit from behind; the mother of a winner. Jean looks over at Canoe.

"Now," she says to Anne, her tone conspiratorial. "What are we going to do about your mother?"

"Ma'am?" Anne says.

"What are we going to do about your—"

"The prize!" Canoe says. "I almost forgot!" She opens her

handbag and pulls out a Japanese fan, the cheap kind bought at any five-and-dime. "Buddy brought this back from Tokyo, the sonofabitch. Told me it belonged to the Empress Hirohito; that she was never supposed to show her face in public." She holds the fan in front of her nose and bats her eyes. "Here's lookin' at you, kid," she says, bowing. "Use it till you learn to lay off the chocolate."

A flush breaks over Anne, reddening her shoulders and arms, inflaming her already inflamed cheeks, though her eyes are set against crying. She leans forward to take the fan from her mother, and as she does her hat slips to the floor. Canoe misunderstands Anne's reach; she grabs Anne in a hug, cinching her as tightly as a belt.

"Well, well," Jean says, picking up her check. "You ladies have a great day."

———

No one remembers who had the idea to drive to Soldier's Field, May Mayhem just beginning. Most likely Canoe led the way in her Woody.

When we got there, boys our girls recognized had already arrived and the girls were immediately gone, pouring out of our cars, discarding their cork sandals to run barefoot on the newly cut grass. Later they strutted about in their floppy hats, suddenly proud of their creations, as if the hats were badges to a secret club. They checked in with us from time to time—for cash or permission—but mostly they were on their own. Who wasn't? And it was fine, after all; they were almost grown. Days like this we'd let ourselves think about it, sober: how we'd done our best, shepherding them from here to there, offering food, shelter, a father they adored, handsome as he was, and various distant relatives. They weren't babies anymore, though in truth we'd trade a thousand days like this one for the feel of them curled on our chests, their tiny toes pushed against our newly soft bellies, their hands fists or splayed.

What we didn't know! We moved blindly through the dark of that, feeling just feet ahead of us; we were sopped in formula, desperate in our good intention. We painted the nursery bright yellow and then changed our minds, to pink. We made lists of what was left to do. But their bodies slipped through our hands, too small they were, when we bathed them, their smell more delicious than anything we had ever tasted. It became enough to see them sleeping, or take a step; to listen to their strange sounds. Then they spoke a word, sentences; they learned to brush their teeth, read their own books. We watched as they walked away from us, *ran* away from us. Good-bye! they yelled, climbing onto the bus as we idled in the parked car, the day too cold to have them standing by themselves—they could catch their death from it! Good-bye! they yelled from the open bus window, we having conceded to stand only at the front door, too far to hear, though we could tell, by the vigorous wave, the pale hand, where they were. We stood long after they'd disappeared—sucked into the bus, sucked into the dappled shadows of the elms, the empty black ribbon of road curling behind them.

No matter. Here was the dawn of Something Big, Canoe said, a shifting of the paradigm. A creative burst! You couldn't not read about it: women in their middle years coming into their own, meeting second husbands, starting businesses, traveling around the globe. We could do any damn thing we liked, Canoe said, unfettered as we were, and we would, we knew, just as soon as we thought what.

But now we think only of the cold. We pull our cardigans from the passenger seat, grab an extra pack of cigarettes. By twilight a breeze picks up, lifting the streamers that hang from the maypole in the center of the field, signaling evening, though the day has stretched on as early spring days will. We huddle on the bleachers among no one we know; soon, we've been told, the dance will begin.

The Hounds, Again

———

Canoe's heard the hounds, again. Not the beagles we sit waiting for, their prissy, wiggling packs, but real hounds, she says, roving, ferocious tribes, their pink collars merely a concession. They circle the poor things, petrify them to stone; it makes the geese infertile to stand cowed in that killer dog's stare, or so it said in the Club newsletter.

It is only a matter of time before the geese lose their fight. You can find their spotty-looking flocks in any one of our fields, or where our fields used to be, their beaks and beady eyes turned to the depths of what was once marsh, their scaly black feet faded to an ashen gray. They sway to and fro, startle easily; if you offer them a handful they flap their wings, as brazen as the seagulls in the Safeway parking lot. More than once we've seen them standing in the middle of the old Route 32, confused.

Get out of our way, they seem to say. "Honk. Honk."

Canoe says that breed will rip the throats of children.

"You're thinking of the German ones," Barbara says. "From the war."

Louise Cooper clears her throat. "Is anyone," she wants to know, "like, listening?"

We laugh, of course, though it's a poor imitation. If you want to capture our daughters you'd have to do this and more: the way they hurry off the phone—busy, busy, busy; roll their eyes; how they twirl their thumbs when we summarize the editorial. They may be kinder now that they have children—we are their tickets to Bermuda, their ski weekend, their night away—but no matter; we've learned to hold our tongues.

Louise has been describing the attempted escape, how He planned to steal out of the Center in the dead of night, His suitcase packed, or as packed as it could be: regulation pajamas, slippers, some sort of shell and glue collage He made in OT. What else? There was apparently a rope woven from the bedspread, floral like our own. We picture Him slipping down a garland of faded roses, hand over hand, holding the suitcase as carefully as Lindbergh's baby.

"Not Rotweillers," Canoe insists. "This kind. They've given them extra training. On rats, or something. I read it; they've taught them cruelty, taught them to tear each other apart. I read it somewhere. Boredom, I think. They bore the things stiff."

We listen to Canoe and then we do not. It's Him we're remembering: Him we will return to: Louise not the only one. He's cornered us all, one after the other, at the children's swim meets, for example, His hair slicked as fine as Gatsby's. He wore swim trunks, a towel around his neck. Did He blow the whistle? Referee? It was a lifetime ago. He smelled of chlorine and coconut, his tan buttery. You could have fried vegetables on that skin, His flavor salt or ginger, a root dug from dirt.

He put His hands on our shoulders, held us still: He our sole transgression.

Somewhere beyond, in the locker room, our daughter hopped foot to foot to get the water out. We imagined her knuckly knees, the dripping stains she made on the poured cement floor. Up from there her horsey, hairy legs rise to a crotch—a *po-po*, we once called it, though now crotch for no other reason than we can't think what else, a vagina? Genitalia? Come on!—newly blurred by hair. We have glimpsed it from time to time, though she hides this from us as she hides her breasts, wearing two, three shirts, her arms crossed even now in our imagining as if she knows she's watched, braces tight with caramel.

He will discover her later as He discovers all the girls, sidle up beside her as He does now to us; she His baby-sitter, the teenager He drives home Saturday nights. Drunk. He finds her sleeping in front of the television, some sort of laugh track too loud though the children are soundly dozing. He stands behind her, smelling of cigarette smoke and indistinguishable booze. (Independence is an important early lesson, we have told ourselves. She's earning pin money, we have said.)

He smooths her shiny hair; she cannot see Him, nor does she wake. She is a dead sleeper. He leans down and breathes in her shampoo: Herbal Essence. He is not blind drunk, but He is close. He should brew coffee, eat something, but He would rather stand here breathing. She smells like all the girls, fourteen, sixteen, the packs of them at the swimming pool, tanning one side and then the other. He forgets their names. They have tiny, pearly teeth encased in metal. They have pink-sheathed eyelids. They rub lemon on their hair and the older ones spritz peroxide from garish-colored bottles. They play their radios although it is against the rules, and from time to time one shrieks as if suddenly bitten.

But now He does not look at her; He looks at us, holds us, even, His eyes a brilliant blue. We think to say it though we think better. It's too corny and besides, there's little time. We are standing in the darker shadow cast by the high noon light. We are hidden if only for an instant within the covered alley to the Lost and Found. He pulls us into Him, His hard cock—it is the only way to say it—His slippery tongue.

We wrap our blankets around our shoulders. Our blankets smell of dog, and when no one's looking we breathe them in, remembering.

But no one's ever looking.

We drain the drink from a sheep gut, squeezing the leather for the last drop. It's frigid, near twenty. Beyond our circle Gay Burt gathers holly from the road ditch. She snips and snips, dropping berry-loaded twigs into the bucket at the base of her high black boots.

She returns now with her stash. "Hail, ye drunkards," she says, walking bucket first. "I say we split, I'm freezing my arse off." Gay Burt opens the door, bucket first. Her hands are scratched and bleeding. There were thorns, and possibly ticks, though it is too cold to worry. In this weather the patches on her nose go white, quilted. She sets the shears on the floor, steps in with her thick boots. The rest of us disperse here and there in our Jeeps, slamming doors, fussing with the dial, the outing somewhat of a failure—they have not yet arrived. And we in truth are halfway gone before we see them; we shut off our engines, roll down the windows. There are no longer any foxes, true—the prissy beagles bark in false pursuit, fooled by something mechanical—but still it is a beautiful sight. We watch as they approach, bounding our old hills on horses saddled and bridled. It is a scene from Wyeth, or earlier, from a different, better century, from Austen—the all of it glazed in tempera: white breath and sleek, black thighs, fine brush strokes for the velvet hard hats, the sweaty, leather girths. The horses heat the day, somehow, and so we idle here in the warmth awhile before turning back to the road.

The children will not come home; we'll have no tree. There is, of course, a story, but who will tell it? Their fathers; the shopping, the grandchildren, the travel. Et cetera, et cetera. They'll be back for Easter, promise. We have our granddaughters' new bonnets tissue-wrapped in the attic, and the candy we bought at discount last year. This a tradition, Easter, the holidays dealt among in-laws and fathers like so many cards, though the game is rigged. We draw a bunny every time—occasionally a turkey. Suffice it to say our Christmas ornaments are intended for the hospice party. We set them to dry across Canoe's mantel, their decorative elements iced with glue: We are not proponents of the straight line.

Gay Burt's is hands down the best: a tiny holly tree, the berries placed as if bulbs, and on the top an angel made from yarn. "I crave red this time of year," she says. "Like grapefruit."

Mimi Klondike struggles with a cattail. She had an idea about a boat, she says, cottonwood sails, but the cottonwood won't comply. She's got nettles sharp as splinters in her fingers. "Damn," she says, taking a drag from her cigarette. Gray ash falls like snow upon her sailboat.

Something's on, one of the movies: *It's a Wonderful Life* or *White Christmas*.

"I used to swoon for Bing," says Bambi.

"That's Jimmy Stewart," says Barbara.

"I know," says Bambi. "I used to swoon for Bing."

"When are we expected?" Suzie wants to know, the invitation delivered over the telephone. Come party with the sick chicks, Judy Sawyer rasped.

Louise Cooper pushes a needle and thread through a felt tree to tack on the tiny dried rose, something from her collection. "What I heard was that a nurse actually saw Him do it; hang there like a lunatic, half in, half out, before He dropped. They said it's not that kind of place. Nobody would have stopped him."

We think of the Center, a brick tudor built by an earlier

DuPont who had, apparently, a bad gene, or several: first one child, then the next. It sprawls at the edge of our town, ringed by ancient maples and rose gardens and a particularly famous grape arbor, its original cuttings directly from the champagne vineyards of Trentino, ironic, since the Center houses mostly drunks, though a wing has been recently renovated for depressives, compulsives, and neurotics. We are not the kind to seek professional assistance. You made your bed, we say. But on certain late afternoons, driving by its maple-lined drive, glimpsing a flash of blue or red light from its upper Tiffany windows—commissioned by a high-ranking Nazi and removed pane by pane from a castle in the Dordogne—we wish for that, for the peacefulness of that, for meals served by well-groomed employees, for the dim lights of chandeliers, and for evenings spent in the company of the unfortunate.

Louise sniffles. "Let Him go, Louise," Barbara says. Still, we all pause to think of Him splayed within those dark maples, His neck cracked.

———

Judy Sawyer is telling us her dream. Lately dreams are what she speaks of; in the last we were back at Esther Curran's, back in the living room with the French-blue divan, the grey-hounds tiny as mice, back at the long table toasting Esther's Walter. Walter was there too, both in his portrait and there, she said, in the way of dreams, and he was beautiful, she said. Stunning; the handsomest husband. How did she do it? Judy asked. That blind happiness? And we did not have an answer.

In this one, Judy's back in Mexico, in that small hotel in Zihuatanejo, the one with the stone steps carved down to the water, or to a cliff overhanging the water. She and Dick had returned for their twentieth anniversary. She used to lie there every day, on that cliff overhanging the water, she says, on a chaise longue, Dick in the hotel bar upstairs doing the crossword. She said she used to lie on that chaise longue every day listening to the water slapping rock, slap slap slap, and thinking that she could just slide right over the edge, slip into the water and drown, and that no one would notice. She told Dick about the feeling, and he attributed it to the dog they had hit and killed in their rental car on the way there from the airport. The dog was one of a number of identical mutts that ran in packs throughout the town, so that every evening when they walked the dusty road into town on their way in for dinner, she would believe that she might see the dog again in that three-legged one, or the one with the ripped ear, though Dick assured her that their dog was dead. I kicked it myself, he said, for she had been the one driving and understandably was too shaken to get out of the car. It suffered nothing, he told her; it was simply alive one second and dead the next.

"That was the beginning of our end," Judy says.

"What do you mean?" Viv says.

"I never told you mine," Judy says.

She looks exhausted and drops back on the pillow. They are all of them, the dying, arranged around the living room: pillows on top of pillows; some from the book group, though most we do not recognize. There are relatives, too, relatives, we assume, and bright-eyed children, washed and combed, clutching packages and wandering toward the Sunshine Room. Judy's daughter, Melissa, is snowbound somewhere, though she'll arrive tomorrow and banish us, as she puts it, to the land of the living. Now Cookie spoons weakened cereal into Judy's mouth. We have, at four o'clock, interrupted dinner.

"So then what happens?" Canoe says.

"What do you mean?" Judy says.

"In your dream?" Canoe says.

"I kill the dog," Judy says.

"What do you mean?" Canoe says.

"It's all I ever do," Judy says.

The illness will soon calcify her larynx. A cruel way to go, Melissa says, though is there any better? In the New Year she will cease to talk, but now it's all she does. We listen to her stories, logical or not. We're all she needs, aren't we? An audience?

Our ornaments dry in our laps; we can feel their weight there. Whiskers we would like to pluck sprout above Judy's lip; her glasses could use a cleaning. Beside her Betsy Croninger wears a knitted cap, her eyebrows undrawn, her dressing gown opened. Someone should button her up.

———

Down the hall in the Sunshine Room they peg the tree together, an eerie artificial blue. Guests watch the male attendants, but the sound is almost a complete silence, the children shushed, the fountain drained for the winter months, the pennies cleared and dropped in the Fund for Refreshment.

Bambi says if it's up to us, it's up to us. She bangs the warped piano, her good hand going as we belt out carols. Behind us our ornaments dangle from the stiff aluminum boughs, their decorative elements askew. We've brought silly hats made of metallic paper; Canoe wears antlers and a red nose. She's been stoned since noon. Still, she sings on key, a member of the church choir for years.

Someone finds a tambourine and Cookie gets down. It might have been her idea, it might have been ours, to form the conga line. We snake around the Sunshine Room, the animals huddled just up the hill, wooly against the gorgeous winter sunset. They've gathered in their manger, built by the male attendants and some heartier guests for warmth: Henrietta the pig and Gus the sheep; the llama, Fitzwilliam. You could almost picture baby Jesus here, beyond the OT ward, wrapped in His swaddling clothes.

———

Canoe drives us back in Bambi's van, handicap and roomy. She's never not our designated driver. We sit two by two like schoolgirls returning from the game. Have we won or lost? Inconsequential, really. We simply return.

Suddenly she sees a flash of something—yellow eyes, fangs. She will tell us all this later. For now she simply swerves the van to the shoulder of the road and stops, whizzing down the windows, shutting off the motor. It is frigid outside and dark; we can see our breathing.

We are on the old Route 32, curvy, eroded by developments, a new sidewalk mandate. West of here is Route 1, the road our children arrive by when they arrive; but there is always traffic, the stop and go of red lights, the mall, the bustle, et cetera, et cetera. We wait for them, east of the strip; an hour from the real airport. Here within our narrow woods, we let the rhododendrons canopy, and the lilac stray to weed. Our homes are hidden by trees and boxwood hedges, forgotten reliquaries, we could tell them, for our kind. But what kind are we? Yellowing pearls on a taut string: valued once but now too fussy. Grit when crushed, we could tell them; we were fakes all along.

———

"I killed a possum once," Canoe says. "Picking Anne up from school; she wouldn't speak to me for a week.

"Its tail was as long as my arm; I'll never forget it. You would have thought I'd run the thing down. Anne acted like I was some kind of monster. It broke my heart, truly," Canoe says. "Not killing the thing. That was an accident. But the way Anne looked at me."

West of here they've banished the dark; you could never lose your way. But here the night is black as pitch. We sit with Canoe, waiting. We have all the time in the world.

The Beginning of the End

Professor Dipple and Cilla Whitney balance together on the edge of the floral sofa, behind them a painting of Rebecca Westerlake, former instructor in biology and Olympic athlete (archery, if memory serves, though it may have been fencing), glaring from her Chair as Winfield Stevens Professor of Economics, Emeritus. She holds a corgi in her lap, the breed favored by the Queen. Nearby, on a Lincoln table, stands a vase of lilies. Orange, her preferred color.

In her lifetime she had been known to wear mismatched kneesocks and to wander from her classroom in the middle of a lecture, a lit cigarette behind her ear. She had met her husband, Carlos, as a Freiburg scholar, he a Spaniard and hopeless at German; they had communicated in Latin, occasionally English. He died soon after they emigrated and was buried in the cemetery adjacent to campus, where she joined him nearly forty years later, their epitaphs indecipherable, poorly carved, though no doubt distinguished and wise. The caretaker appointed by the college still, on Memorial Day, stuck a flag near the spot where their coffins touched, mistakenly believing him a veteran of the Great War, though in truth the war had been Civil, and in Spain. Still, it gave Carlos something to do, the twirling, since the Massachusetts wind, even in late May, could be fierce, and they were on the highest peak, Professor Westerlake commanding the best real estate in death as she did in life—the house where she had lived alone for decades, a Georgian on the corner of Main and East, still referred to simply as Westerlake.

———

Now Viv stares as if attempting to will Professor Westerlake down from her Chair, as if, with enough concentration, the corgi might yelp and leap from her lap, intent on the door, slightly ajar, by which the three have entered just a short while ago. The original idea had been to take a walk, though rain had interrupted that, and so now they found themselves in the Ladies' Study Room, deserted, exams over for days. In fact Viv's bags are packed and ready to go, waiting at the bottom of the long, elegant staircase that leads to her room, or what has been her room for several years. She had requested, and been given, a single, anticipating even before she arrived on the campus her isolation, or rather, her separateness from the other girls.

Why Professor Dipple and Cilla Whitney had suggested the outing, and what they intended to say to her, was abundantly clear, though they both seemed tongue-tied. So Viv had for some time been making the kind of idle conversation that made them all uncomfortable. On their walk she pointed out the various buildings in which she had taken classes, pointed to the window in the library behind which, she explained, stood her carrel, or what she considered to be her carrel, since there were no appointed carrels, as they must know, but everyone—and by this she meant the girls— just claimed one for themselves at the start of the year, though since she had stayed through summers she had kept hers for four, which was practically unheard of, so that now, really, she thought of it almost as if it were her office, or her private study, and she couldn't imagine who might occupy it next and when she did it made her terribly depressed (it was a new word for Viv, one she had picked up in her psychology seminar and now used with abandon).

That she went on and on about the carrel embarrassed Viv, and she cut herself off abruptly after the word *depressed*. Still, she couldn't help but think about it, walking in the light drizzle with the two of them, how she had put up photographs of her brothers, and a new one, this spring, of Don, and how she would sit there through most nights until the other girls were already back in their rooms, or the smoking rooms, gossiping or whatnot, in the quiet, looking out that window to the view.

———

Viv has run out of drivel and the rain leaves her tired, besides. She looks down and fingers the ring Don presented her last week; it still feels too large, though in truth it is small, a thin gold band with a tiny Empire diamond.

Cilla Whitney leans forward. Viv sits across from the two of them in an uncomfortable, straight-back chair.

"We wanted to talk to you about your career," Cilla Whitney says.

The word *career* lifts and flaps around the room, then settles on Rebecca Westerlake's shoulder; it caws and pecks her face, but she doesn't flinch. She is dead now and has had it with choices, death comforting for that, at least. It was all an impossible decision, wasn't it? But easier, somehow, in her day.

"Yes?" Viv says; she knows exactly, of course.

Cilla Whitney smiles; she must have, at one time, been a beautiful girl. Everyone says it. She has green eyes accentuated with black paint, and a way of holding her head at an angle that gives the appearance of even greater height, though she is tall. She came to Smith to teach dance, studied with Isadora Duncan, or possibly Martha Graham, in San Francisco—there was a story about Salvador Dali as well, though Viv can't remember the details—and soon moved on to dean of students. That she was Dipple's companion was the source of much discussion, since Professor Dipple seemed mostly sexless, androgynous in her heavy shoes, her large, square hands, the way her voice rang out in class.

Now Cilla Whitney turns to Professor Dipple, who sits childlike beside her, as if someone has come along and propped her up on the floral sofa. Of the two, Professor Dipple is clearly the more awkward; understandably, since she spends her days either alone in her office or behind the lectern at a great distance from her students. Cilla Whitney talked all day, or that's what she would say whenever asked her profession. I talk all day, she said. Talk, talk, talk. No, but really, I adore the girls. Just talk, talk, talk.

"We understand you've withdrawn your application for the graduate scholarship," Professor Dipple says, her voice surprisingly direct. "Or, I should say, have requested a deferral."

"I thought it would be better to wait a year," Viv says. "To give myself some time to think."

This is not entirely untrue, or rather, this is what she has been telling herself since the day before yesterday, when she walked into the president's office and requested that Mrs. Brown, the secretary for such matters, remove her application from the thick pile marked "Scholarship Apps" that she could see, even from where she stood. She pictured Professor Dipple and President Macabe reading her essay and blushed, remembering the care she had taken with it, how she had even footnoted a few references, particularly that one to Wallace Stevens—"I was the world in which I walked, and what I saw / Or heard or felt came not but from myself; / And there I found myself more truly and more strange"— and had she been so stupid as to title the thing, as if Professor Dipple and President Macabe were reading an original work, a thing worthy of a title, as if they might later reference it or think back to something insightful she had said?

The world will not mourn the loss of another scholar of modernism, she thinks; the world will particularly not mourn the loss of her as another scholar of modernism.

Professor Dipple lets out her breath

"The department meets today. Cilla and I believe whomever we suggest would be a serious candidate. If you'll reconsider."

Years later, when Viv thought about it—this moment in May, this hour—she wondered how she must have looked to them. No more a woman than a toad, her letter jacket heavy on her shoulders. She sat with legs crossed at the ankles and smoothed her lap. She had difficulty looking straight at Dipple's eyes, their violet blue, and chose her heavy gray eyebrows instead. Dipple wore the dark suit she tended to wear for class, a man's button-down dress shirt tucked in at the waist. Her shoes were heavy, though Viv could not quite see her feet, tucked, as they were, beneath the coffee table between them.

"Well," she says—there was no good way to do it—"the truth is I've decided to get married.

"First," she adds.

The bird on Rebecca Westerlake's shoulder caws and flaps its wings, its ugly, pink eyes shrinking. She could be a portrait, couldn't she? Isn't that what Don had said? Living out her days with a dog and a bunch of dusty women? Not that she had expressed much indecision. The thought of him proposing sent a flush through her hot to cold even now— the way he walked his fingers over her knee, held her hand. He had given her the ring just last week, and she'd said yes, of course; the question one that seemed, just by the asking, to demand the affirmative. She was going to be married. She was: Here she had just told them and here it was again true, just as it became true every time she said it, first to her aunt Sara, who fanned herself and took a seat, and then to her brothers, who slapped Don's back, or the equivalent, and then to her father, who looked at her as if he'd never noticed she was a girl.

Still, through all of the telling she had felt a certain duplicity to the news, as if it were both true and untrue, felt it was a game of sorts she played, a mass of twine she twisted into a form that she could easily unravel. She could say yes, and then she could say no. Depending. At this moment, right now, she said yes because she wore the ring, because Don was due to pick her up at five o'clock, and because they would drive straight to her aunt Sara's house, where an engagement party had been planned, her relatives arriving from Pittsburgh. That she would graduate on Saturday seemed beside the point.

———

Neither Cilla Whitney nor Professor Dipple says a word, though the looks on their faces Viv will never know, since Viv does not take her own eyes off her knees until the looks are rearranged, composed into better looks, or rather, looks that Viv will not understand for years.

"Well," Professor Dipple says at last. "I can't say I'm not disappointed."

"He's got a job with Johnson & Johnson. Sales. Apparently we'll relocate every few years."

"So you need time to think," Professor Dipple says.

"They've even got a plant in Brussels!"

"Screw and think," Dipple says.

The word rips through the scene—window looking out to central quad, a rainy day; sends the props—silver tea set, Lincoln table, Turkish rug—spinning.

"Brussels!" Cilla Whitney says.

"I might take a few classes here and there," Viv continues. "Don's comfortable with the idea."

"*He's* comfortable?" Professor Dipple says.

"Well, he seems to be now. I'll keep my fingers crossed. And then next year, I'll apply again—"

"Oh, you do just that," Professor Dipple says. "You keep your fingers crossed."

"Charlotte," Cilla Whitney says, and it is the first time Viv has ever heard Dipple's given name, entirely wrong, like a lace coverlet on a steel bed.

Professor Dipple leans forward and fixes her stare on Viv. It is a stare Viv has seen countless times, though it has never, before this moment, been directed at her; rather at the girl who seems restless in her seat, or the one who answers the question idiotically. Then Professor Dipple curls her fingers around the depression meant for pens in the lectern and stares until the girl settles in her seat and straightens her shoulders (the proper posture, Dipple had announced the first day of class, for intellection), or the girl rephrases her answer and responds with some semblance of insight.

Professor Dipple suffers no fools. She has been known, in certain moods, to abandon a class altogether, to walk out, leaving the girls lined up like so many dunces, staring at whatever notes she might have left on the blackboard.

Viv feels winded by the look, by the vulgarity of the word *screw*, by Dipple's fury; she feels suddenly thrown off the course she has so carefully followed since Don proposed, tacking back and forth, sure to get there despite the emptiness of the horizon.

"Do you know what they'll ask you at any serious institution if they find out you're a married woman? Are you pregnant? they'll say. Do you plan on getting pregnant? What kind of birth control are you using? And believe me, if you say something as idiotic as the rhythm method, they'll throw you out on your ear."

"You would like him," Viv says.

"I'm sure," Cilla Whitney says.

"You might very well read a book from time to time," Dipple continues, "but you will not read it in the way that matters; the constellation will disappear, the connections you make now as a young scholar. It will all fade into fuzzy thinking."

Viv could laugh—fuzzy thinking—or cry, because it seemed to be happening already, or since the moment she said, Yes. How can she explain it? At times she would like to return to where, or who, she was before she met Don, the girl who stayed in her library carrel, who took notes, writing so carefully, pressing so deep into the lined paper that she often tore it, so that a sentence copied from one of her books, or from the notes she took in shorthand in class—the wise things her teachers said—had holes straight through.

Still, the all of it remained there, beginning to end; the words on the page, even in her clunky script, like beautifully carved steps to a place where everything was promised to be clear. She simply needed to climb.

But she has somehow lost her footing; and now she wallows in a place unnameable. She loves him, doesn't she? Yes, she does. She loves him and she will marry him in less than a month, the ring he gave her just last week—a thin gold band with a tiny Empire diamond—the very one his mother had worn, and her mother before her. What did Cilla Whitney and Charlotte Dipple know of this? What did they know of any of it? Of the way he walked his fingers up her knee? Held her hand?

"There's some time," Viv says. "I'll think about it," she says, though she's not entirely sure what she means by "it."

Professor Dipple stands and walks to the window, and her shoes are indeed hard, orthopedic, her dark suit wrinkled in the back; she seems old, suddenly, her disappointment bottomless: a *refugee*.

———

If she had been less shy, or less stupid, Viv will remember, she might have stood and walked over to Dipple, told her of how, sometimes, she read her notes from Dipple's class aloud just to hear the sound of Dipple's words in her own voice. But she did not stand, she simply watched the rain out the window from her place on the straight-back chair. It came down so hard that the view of the campus appeared washed away. Perhaps there had never been a campus at all, a carrel where she would sit most Saturday nights, copying notes, wishing, she could tell them now, shout at them, for nothing more than a boy like Don to invite her to the movies. And that's exactly what he'd done; invited her to the movies, *High Noon*, and in the dark his fingers had walked up her bare knee, and he had held her hand and afterward he had invited her to the game and after that he had invited her to dinner and after that he had sat with her here, on campus, in the quad designated for mixing and they had smoked cigarettes and talked of their plans and he had said, just like that, Will you marry me?

And she had said yes.

Because, what else?

What possibly else?

And now she was going to be late, and he would be waiting for her in the house where she had lived alone for nearly four years, and she still had some packing before leaving and the party—an engagement party Aunt Sara had originally intended as a graduation party, but she had altered the theme, she said, for obvious reasons when she heard the news— would already be starting, relatives coming all the way from Pittsburgh. What did they know of any of it, Cilla Whitney and Professor Dipple? How all the women in her family already stood in the receiving line, had stood there from the moment she was born—her mother, dead a year now, Aunt Sara, her grandmother—extreme in their expectation, in their suffering, as they waited for her to say yes. All they had ever wanted, it seemed, was for her to say yes.

So yes, she said. Yes.
"I'm sorry," Viv says.
Dipple turns from the window.
"As am I," she says.

———

Dipple puts on her reading glasses. They'd better continue, rain or not, since the department meeting would soon begin, she says. They leave the Ladies' Study Room through the same door through which they had entered, quickly saying good-byes in the hallway. And who's to ever know whether Rebecca Westerlake shook her head or stretched her arms after they'd gone? Who's to know whether anything has been disrupted by their conversation, or whether everything remains exactly as it has always been: Rebecca Westerlake square in her frame, her corgi perched on her lap like a small child, a vase of orange lilies balanced behind.

———

Viv must hurry now. If she stopped to consider it, she would realize that she will never see Professor Dipple again, Dipple by tradition refusing to march with the other faculty at commencement, believing the pomp and circumstance fascistic. But Viv does not stop to consider it; she thinks only of Don, of how he does not like to wait and how anxious he'll be to begin their drive before dark.

She turns down the muddy path that shortcuts north

quad and begins through a grove of birch, a memorial to someone, bordered by a rose garden and a low stone wall. She slows some, as if suddenly burdened, or lightened, her mind as changeable as the weather, the rain letting up to nothing more than a mist. It would be easier if she were more like the other girls, the ones who might have been friends—the hours they spent talking about the boys they were dating, the boys they wanted to date, how this one just got pinned, how this one expected a ring by spring. Shouldn't she be? The others, the ones who never mentioned boys at all, were so odd, so already lonely. Her own company seemed better than theirs, better than anyone's, actually.

The wet birch leaves, newly green, reflect the light. There's a sunset somewhere, or the colors of one, if you look. Viv stops, her shoes soaked through. She could step back. She could, even now, turn around and run, burst into the department meeting to announce that she changed her mind, that she'll accept the scholarship after all! (She pictures an apartment in some distant, crowded city, a stack of books and a coffeepot, unanswered letters and photographs of nieces and nephews, a cat on the sill; there are sheer white curtains that blow in with a late breeze, and the sun on the white-painted wall casts a stark shadow; is she here, then? Is this where she belongs? In a separate room, perhaps? Reading in a corner?)

But now the women reappear: her mother as she was in death, her rage at life no more hidden by the rouge and face paint than a third eye. She stares out from within the satin coffin lining, glasses perched on her nose as if somebody's idea of a joke. Viv had thought there might be peace for her here, but clearly Mother had found none. Viv took her seat in the front row, the funeral director flicking the hidden switch that closed the curtain, the coffin whisked away as the minister, a man recommended by the funeral home, read a poem Mother had always loved from *Good Housekeeping*—something about a vacuum cleaner.

Aunt Sara. Grandmother.

These women are the precedent, the breathing, disapproving antecedent. They know full well the way it will go for her but they will not say a word of warning, rather they lead her to it like a lamb to slaughter, their mouths drawn as if with string and knotted tight; character destiny? Pshaw. Biology destiny. Their characters, they could tell you, were flawless, or once so, they tried and tried again, learned good manners, spoke when spoken to, kept a neat house. But there is little strength in numbers; no company in misery. They simply stand in their line, side by side, waiting—she can almost feel their hot breath—for her to join them, to step in.

And she will, of course, join them. She has never had any choice in the matter; it has been laid out for her, encoded in her cells like the pattern on the bone china handed down and handed down, again. Life as it will be for women: first the husband, thin legs and big hands, a way of correcting in small then larger ways—directions, instructions, certain ways of behaving—and then the children, their sparrow throats veiny from birth, opened for worms, chattering, screeching, wings wet and folded against their bony bodies until they have eaten enough to fly, the nest she has made for them downy at first, as if in a picture book, cotton-filled, soft, then hardening with time, the thorns hidden within the cotton seed, the red-brown twigs and sharp nettles there all along.

Deferred, she had once thought. A year or two of waiting; then she would show them what a woman could do.

―――

At dinner parties men speak in declarative sentences of things she has no interest in, or better, the corners of the world she has conceded to them: monetary systems, foreign debts, company matters. She likes a good discussion and waits to be asked, though she'll take any crumbs. There is so much to arrange! she says to an inquiry. The children's school year starts on Tuesday!

Then one afternoon she climbs the attic steps to read through her old notebooks, the black-rimmed announcement of Professor Dipple's death in that month's alumnae bulletin a shock to her, somehow, though of course it's been years and years. Survived, the obituary read, by her longtime companion, Cilla Whitney, former dean of students and now retired and living in Newport, Rhode Island. Viv thinks of Cilla Whitney there, on a bluff, still beautiful. She imagines Professor Dipple walking along the rocky shore—she hadn't thought of her in years!—dressed in her man's suit, her hard shoes. She weeps for all of them, deciding, at that moment, to enroll in one of the community college adult offerings. She settles for a writing class entitled "Finding the Plot (or Point?) of Your Story."

The instructor is a young man named Gordon, fresh from graduate school, a novelist, he tells them, though he has not yet published a book. He encourages her, the oldest in the room, to be brave, to stand and read her sentences with, as he says, all the gusto she can muster. She holds her notebook at a height that will bring her letters into focus—the damned earnestness of it all, she's already thinking, the pretension of the very act—and begins to read, too quickly, she knows, and with too much pride, though she cannot keep the emotion out of her voice. It is this way for all of us, isn't it? Viv thinks. Canoe, Bambi, Mimi, Judy Sawyer, Louise, Suzie, Barbara, even Esther, before, in her manner: The few times we speak of true things it is almost unbearable, and so we do not, mostly, preferring to laugh.

The class listens for a few moments as she reads and then Viv hears the terrible shift in the silence, knowing full well the sound of inattention. It doesn't matter the seriousness of the words or the sentiments; she has arranged them wrong, failed to give them the form they took in her mind so that even she can hear the breath in them, the weightlessness: They float above her head and pop like so many soap bubbles; she casts out air and she had meant for, what? Arrows? Bullets? At one time, she could tell them, she had been full of sharp things, tricky corners and footholds and craggy, jagged peaks to grab, to ascend, but now that place is lost to her, the door closed. Fuzzy thinking. Viv looks up to see Professor Dipple way in the back, as bored as the rest of them. Dipple hunches in her chair and scratches her knee. "I'm sorry," Viv mouths and Dipple shrugs as if to say, Don't be.

Gordon interrupts and asks Viv to read the last sentence again, more slowly. "Hmm," he says; then suggests she aim for something a little different next time around; that she write of "barbed things."

"Such as fishhooks?" she says, intending humor.

He strokes his mustache, or what would be a mustache in an older man.

"Possibly," he says.

She takes her seat and looks around the room; a few of the younger women smile. One young boy with a ponytail gives her the thumbs-up. Dipple, however, has disappeared, replaced by an empty chair.

———

The next week Gordon nods as Viv reads, but she pays little attention: The fire is out; the passion faded; she did not impress him, nor anyone, for that matter. She did not shine as she had imagined and there are weeks to go.

"When I listen to your words," he says slowly after she has finished, "I think of flowers."

"Yes?" she says, her heart oddly fluttering, hopeful.

"Entire gardens," he says, "in your lines."

The word *lines* calls to mind not her sentences, as he no doubt intended, but the very definition of her body, the limits of her arms and legs—her silhouette, her shadow, the way she appears to the world. The lumpiness of her now, the ungainly extremities: her skin gone prickly, her bones already softening, bending, her hair thin and colored. A woman of a certain age, tucked into panel stockings, zipped in wool or cotton, warmed by a sweater or, on certain days, a silk scarf. At times she is even painted—red lips, bronze eyelids, a thin, black line within the lashes—to be presentable. But perhaps he sees, or rather hears, what others miss; what she has always known: There are gardens here, gorgeous, complicated landscapes.

"Yes?" she says.

He smiles, again, and nods. "I wanted fishhooks," he says.

"Oh," she says.

"Bloody, scaly barbs," he says.

"Right," she says.

Viv will skip the rest of the semester though Gordon will call to check in, leaving a message that he is sorry if he was discouraging, that he thought she had some beautiful imagery. An ear for language.

Don startles her so she nearly screams. He's in the middle of the path and she hasn't been looking. He wears a gray raincoat and he is short; she had forgotten. She is nearly his height, shoulder to shoulder, though this is their only resemblance. Where she is dark, he is pale, bleached. He has practically no eyelashes, so that at times he takes on what she thinks of as a bumpy, snakey look, a particularity which now she merely notes as she notes all particularities (Professor Dipple had once told her that *noticing* was all the proof she needed of her textured inner life), though in time it will grow so disturbing that she will find she has difficulty looking at him, believing, at any moment, his tongue might dart the air. But his hands! Smooth as milk; they wrap his umbrella—in his concern he hasn't noticed that the rain has stopped, that the sun shines. He holds the umbrella out toward her and his smile belies the sternness of his voice. He's been waiting for nearly an hour, he is saying. He'd begun to get worried.

"Worried?" she says. "What could possibly have happened to me?"

She tilts her face toward his and kisses him. The receiving line of women exhale, their lips relaxing into the dull smiles found in cameos. They will fade from Viv's mind, reappearing only in certain predictable situations—when things go well for her, when things go badly. But for now they are banished and she is here, alone, with her fiancé, a man she will marry next month.

She moves in closer to Don and bumps the umbrella, its slick sides dripping on their shoulders as they kiss beneath the dome, already bound. And there will never be a stepping back, nor a fork in the road, nor a deferral of what had been a clear direction. You made your bed, the women say, et cetera, et cetera.

This is how Viv would describe, if asked, the beginning of the end, but the conversation never gets around to her.